"Do you still love him?"

She was poleaxed. "What?"

Noah was in front of her in three steps. "Your fiancé…do you still love him?"

"He's dead," she whispered.

"I know. But that wasn't the question." He reached for her, slid one arm around her waist and drew her against him. "The thing is," he said, holding her firm. "If you still love him…I'll do my best to stop…to stop wanting you." His other hand cupped her cheek, gently, carefully. "But if you don't love him, then I'd really like to kiss you right now."

Her insides contracted. "No," she said on a breath.

"No?"

"I don't love him."

His green eyes darkened as he traced his thumb along her jaw. "Good," he said softly.

And then he kissed her.

Dear Reader,

I have always been a sucker for old romance movies and corny love songs. It seemed an obvious choice then, when I decided to be a writer at the age of seven that I would write romance. Of course, back then it was about love between a girl and her horse, but I was on the right track.

Horses have always been a big part of my life and several years ago I married a single dad, and because both those themes are a big part of this story, I'm delighted that *Made For Marriage* is my first book published with Harlequin Special Edition. I hope you enjoy Noah & Callie's journey and I invite you to return to Crystal Point very soon.

I would love to hear from readers and can be reached via my website, www.helenlacey.com.

Warmest wishes,

Helen Lacey

MADE FOR MARRIAGE

HELEN LACEY

Harlequin

SPECIAL EDITION

Recycling programs
for this product may
not exist in your area.

ISBN-13: 978-0-373-65648-6

MADE FOR MARRIAGE

Books by Helen Lacey

Harlequin Special Edition

Made for Marriage #2166

HELEN LACEY

grew up reading *Black Beauty, Anne of Green Gables* and *Little House on the Prairie*. These childhood classics inspired her to write her first book when she was seven years old, a story about a girl and her horse. She continued to write with the dream of one day being a published author, and writing for Harlequin Special Edition is the realization of that dream. She loves creating stories about strong heroes with a soft heart and heroines who get their happily-ever-after. For more about Helen, visit her website, www.helenlacey.com.

For Robert
Emphatically, Undeniably, Categorically.

ACKNOWLEDGMENTS

To the Babes
Louise Cusack, Lesley Millar, Laura O'Connell,
CC Coburn & the amazing Helen Bianchin.
Thank you for your endless support.

To my editor, Susan Litman, and my agent, Scott Eagan,
who both trusted in my storytelling.

And to Valerie Susan Hayward—
for showing me how it's done.

Chapter One

Callie Jones knew trouble when she came upon it. And the thirteen-year-old who stood defiantly in front of her looked like more trouble than she wanted on a Saturday morning. For one thing, Callie liked to sleep later on the weekend, and the teenager with the impudent expression had banged on her door at an indecently early 6:00 a.m. And for another, the girl wasn't anything like she'd expected. Her long black hair was tied up in an untidy ponytail revealing at least half a dozen piercings in her ears, plus another in both her brow and nose. And the dark kohl smudged around her eyes was heavier than any acceptable trend Callie had ever seen.

"I'm Lily," the girl said, crossing her thin arms. "I'm here for my lesson."

Callie opened the front door fractionally, grateful she'd had the sense to wrap herself in an old dressing gown before she'd come to the door. It was chilly outside. "You're early," she said, spotting a bicycle at the bottom of the steps.

The teenager shrugged her shoulders. "So what? I'm here now."

Callie hung on to her patience. "I told your father eight o'clock."

Lily shrugged again, without any apology in her expression. "Then I guess he told me the wrong time." The girl looked her over, and Callie felt the burning scrutiny right down to her toes.

Callie took a deep breath and glanced over the girl's head. Dawn was just breaking on the horizon. Another hour of sleep would have been nice, but she wasn't about to send Lily home.

"Okay, Lily. Give me a few minutes to get ready." Callie pointed to the wicker love seat on the porch. "Wait here. I'll be right back."

The girl shrugged. "Whatever."

Callie locked the security mesh screen as discreetly as she could and turned quickly on her heels. She didn't want an unsupervised teenager wandering around her house while she changed her clothes. Dashing into the bathroom, she washed her face and brushed her teeth and hair before slipping into jeans and a T-shirt.

She skipped coffee, grabbed a cereal bar and shoved it into her back pocket. She really needed to do some grocery shopping. But she was too busy. Busy with her students, busy trying to ensure the utilities were paid, busy not thinking about why a recently turned thirty ex-California girl worked twelve-hour days trying to make a success of a small horse-riding school situated a few miles from the eastern edge of the Australian coastline.

Callie grabbed her sweater from the back of the kitchen chair and headed for the front door. Once she'd locked up she pulled her muddy riding boots off the shoe rack, quickly tucked her feet into them, snatched up her battered cowboy hat and placed it on her head. She turned around to find no sign of her visitor. Or the expensive-looking bicycle.

Obviously the teenager wasn't keen on following instructions.

She put the keys into her pocket and headed for the stables. The large stable complex, round yard and dressage arena were impressive. Callie had spent nearly every penny she had on Sandhills Farm to ensure it became a workable and viable business.

Okay kid—where are you?

Tessa rushed from around the back of the house. Still a pup, the Labrador/cattle dog cross bounded on lanky legs and yapped excitedly. Obviously no kid was back there, or Tessa would have hung around for attention.

So, where was she? Callie's intuition and instincts surged into overdrive. Miss Too-Many-Piercings was clearly looking for trouble. She called the girl's name. No answer.

When Callie opened the stable doors and flicked the lock mechanism into place, a few long heads immediately poked over the stalls. She looked around and found no sign of Lily.

Great—the kid had gone AWOL.

And where on earth was Joe, her farmhand? She checked her watch. Six-twenty-five. He was late and she'd have to attend to the feeding before she could start the lesson with her missing student.

First things first—find Lily…um…whatever-her-last-name-is. She clicked her fingers together. Hah—Preston. That's right. Lily Preston.

She's got the father with the sexy telephone voice, remember?

Callie shook some sense into her silly head when she heard a vehicle coming down the driveway. Joe…good. She swiveled on her heel and circumnavigated the stables, stopping abruptly, mid-stride, too stunned to move.

Indiana—her beautiful, precious and irreplaceable Hanoverian gelding—stood by the fence, wearing only an ill-fitting bridle. Lily Preston was straddled between the fence post and trough as she attempted to climb onto his back.

Think...and think quickly.

Callie willed her legs to move and raced toward the girl and horse, but it was too late. The teenager had mounted, collected the reins and clicked the gelding into a trot Callie knew she would have no hope of sustaining.

She's going to fall. And before Callie had a chance to move, Lily Preston lost control, tumbled off the horse and landed squarely on her behind.

She was gone. Ditto for her bike. Noah Preston cursed and headed back into the house. The last thing he'd told his angry daughter the night before, just as she'd slammed her bedroom door in his face, was that he'd take her to Sandhills Farm at seven-forty-five in the morning. She hadn't wanted him to take her. She wanted to go alone. Without him. He should have taken more notice. The time was now six-thirty-three and Lily had skipped. In typical Lily style.

"Daddy, I'm hungry."

Noah turned his head. His eight-year-old son, Jamie, as uncomplicated and placid a child as Lily was not, stood in the doorway.

"Okay," he said. "I'll make breakfast soon. But we have to go find Lily first."

Jamie rolled his big eyes. "Again?"

Noah smiled. "I know, mate, but I have to make sure she's safe."

"She is," Jamie assured him in a very grown-up fashion. "She's gone to see the horse lady."

"She told you that?"

His son nodded. "Yep. Told me this morning. She rode her bike. I told her not to."

The horse lady? *Callie Jones.* Recommended as the best equestrian instructor in the district. He'd called her a week ago, inquiring about setting Lily up with some lessons. Her soft, American accent had intrigued him and he'd quickly made arrangements to bring Lily out to her riding school.

So, at least he knew where she'd gone and why. To make a point. To show him he had no control, no say, and that she could do whatever she pleased.

Noah spent the following minutes waking the twins and making sure the three kids were clothed, washed and ready to leave. Jamie grumbled a bit about being hungry, so Noah grabbed a few apples and a box of cereal bars for the trip. He found his keys, led his family outside, bundled the children into his dual-cab utility vehicle and buckled them up.

He lived just out from Crystal Point and the trip took barely ten minutes. Sandhills Farm was set back from the road and gravel crunched beneath the wheels when he turned off down the long driveway. He followed the line of white-washed fencing until he reached the house, a rundown, big, typical Queenslander with a wraparound veranda and hatbox roof. Shabby but redeemable.

So where was Lily?

He put Jamie in charge of four-year-old Hayley and Matthew, took the keys from the ignition and stepped out of the vehicle. A dog came bounding toward him, a happy-looking pup that promptly dropped to Noah's feet and pleaded for attention. Noah patted the dog for a moment, flipped off his sunglasses and looked around. The house looked deserted. An old Ford truck lay idle near the stables and he headed for it. The keys hanging in the ignition suggested someone was around. He spotted Lily's bicycle propped against the wall of the stable. So she *was* here.

But where? And where was Callie Jones? He couldn't see a sign of anyone in the yards or the stables or in the covered sand arena to the left of the building. The stable doors were open and he took a few steps inside, instantly impressed by the setup. A couple of horses tipped their heads over the top of their stalls and watched him as he made his way through. He found the tack room and small office at the end of the row of stalls. The door was ajar and he tapped on the jamb. No one answered. But he could see inside. There were pictures on the wall—all of horses in varying competitive poses. The rider in each shot was female. Perhaps Callie Jones?

Noah lingered for another few seconds before he returned outside. The friendly dog bounded to his feet again, demanding notice. The animal stayed for just a moment before darting past him and heading off around the side of the building. Noah instructed the kids to get out of the truck and told them to follow him. As he walked with the three children in a straight line behind him, he heard the sound of voices that got louder with every step. When he turned another corner he stopped. The breath kicked from his chest.

A woman stood by the fence.

Was this Callie Jones? Not too tall, not too thin. Curves every place a woman ought to have them. Her jeans, riding low, looked molded onto her hips and legs. Long brown hair hung down her back in a ponytail and his fingers itched with the thought of threading them through it. Noah's heart suddenly knocked against his ribs. *Lightning,* he thought. *Is this what it feels like to be struck by lightning?*

Noah probably would have taken a little more time to observe her if he hadn't spotted his daughter sitting on the ground, her clothes covered in dust and a big brown horse looming over her.

* * *

"What's going on here?"

Callie jumped and turned around on her heels.

A man glared at her from about twenty feet away.

"Hey, Dad," called Lily.

Uh-oh. The father? He looked *very* unhappy. Callie switched her attention back to the girl sitting on the ground. She was sure Lily's butt would be sore for a day or so. And she was thankful Indiana had stopped once he'd realized his inexperienced rider was in trouble. Which meant all that had really happened was Lily had slipped off the side. It wasn't a serious fall. And she intended to tell him so.

Callie wiped her hands down her jeans. "Hi, I'm—"

"Lily," he barked out, interrupting her and bridging the space between them with a few strides. "What happened?"

She made a face. "I fell off."

"She's okay," Callie said quickly.

"I think I'll decide that for myself," he said and helped his daughter to her feet.

Lily dusted off her clothes and crossed her thin arms. "I'm fine, Dad."

Indiana moved toward Callie and nuzzled her elbow. "Good boy," she said softly, patting his nose.

"You're rewarding him for throwing my daughter?"

Heat prickled up her spine. "He didn't throw her."

Silence stretched like elastic between them as he looked at her with the greenest eyes Callie had ever seen. It took precisely two seconds to register he was attractive. It didn't matter that he scowled at her. She still had enough of a pulse to recognize an absolutely gorgeous man when faced with one. If she were looking. Which she wasn't.

Then she saw children behind him. A lot of children. Three. All blond.

A familiar pain pierced behind her rib cage.

"Lily, take the kids and go and wait by the truck."

"But, Dad—"

"Go," he instructed.

Callie clutched Indiana's reins tightly. Gorgeous, maybe. Friendly, not one bit.

His daughter went to say something else but stopped. She shrugged her shoulders and told the smaller children to follow her. Once Lily and the children were out of sight the man turned to her. "What exactly do you think you were doing?"

"I was—"

"My daughter gets thrown off a horse and you just left her lying in the dirt. What if she'd been seriously injured?"

Callie held her ground. She'd handled parents before. "She wasn't, though."

"Did you even check? I'll see your license revoked," he said. "You're not fit to work with children."

That got her mouth moving. "Just wait one minute," she said, planting her hands on her hips for dramatic effect. "You don't have the right—"

"I do," he said quickly. "What kind of nut are you?"

Callie's face burned. "I'm not a—"

"Of all the irresponsible things I've—"

"Would you stop interrupting me," she said, cutting him off right back. It did the trick because he clammed up instantly. He really was remarkably handsome. Callie took a deep breath. "Your daughter took my horse without permission."

"So this is Lily's fault?"

"I didn't say that."

He stepped closer and Callie was suddenly struck by how tall he was and how broad his shoulders were. "Then it's your fault?" He raised his hands. "Your property, your horse…it's not hard to figure out who's to blame."

"She took the horse without my permission," Callie said

again, firmer this time, making a point and refusing to be verbally outmaneuvered by a gorgeous man with a sexy voice.

His green eyes glittered. "So she was wandering around unsupervised, Ms. Jones?"

Annoyance weaved up her spine. *Ms. Jones? Nothing friendly about that.*

She took a deep breath and willed herself to keep her cool. "I understand how this looks and how you must feel, but I think—"

"Are you a parent?" he asked quickly.

"No."

"Then you don't know how I feel."

He was right—she didn't have a clue. She wasn't a parent. She'd never be a parent. Silence stretched. She looked at him. He looked at her. Something flickered between them. An undercurrent. Not of anger—this was something else.

He's looking at me. He's angry. He's downright furious. But he's checking me out.

Callie couldn't remember the last time she'd registered that kind of look. Or the last time she'd wanted to look back. But she knew she shouldn't. He had children. He was obviously married. She glanced at his left hand. *No wedding ring.* Her belly dipped nonsensically.

His eyes narrowed. "Have you any qualifications?"

She stared at him. "I have an instructor's ticket from the Equestrian Federation of—"

"I meant qualifications to work with kids?" he said, cutting off her ramble. "Like teaching credentials? Or a degree in child psychology? Come to think of it, do you have any qualifications other than the fact you can ride a horse?"

Outraged, Callie opened her mouth to speak but quickly stopped. She was suddenly tongue-tied, stripped of her usual ability to speak her mind. Her cheeks flamed and thankfully her silence didn't last long. "Are you always so...so rude?"

He smiled as though he found her anger amusing. "And do you always allow your students to walk around unsupervised?"

"No," she replied, burning up. "But you're not in possession of all the facts."

He watched her for a moment, every gorgeous inch of him focused on her, and she experienced a strange dip in the pit of her stomach, like she was riding a roller coaster way too fast.

"Then please...enlighten me," he said quietly.

Callie bit her temper back. "When Lily arrived early I told her to wait for me. She didn't."

"And that's when she took your horse?"

"Yes."

"Why didn't you tell her to get off?"

"I did," Callie replied. "Although I've discovered that sometimes its better practice to let people find out just how—"

"You mean the hard way?" he asked, cutting her off again.

Callie nodded. "But she wasn't in any danger. Indiana wouldn't have hurt her."

"Just for the record," he said quietly—so quietly Callie knew he was holding himself in control—"Lily knows all about hard life lessons."

She's not the only one.

Good sense thankfully prevailed and she kept her cool. "I'm sorry you had a reason to be concerned about her safety," she said quietly. "I had no idea she would do something like that."

"Did it occur to you to call me?" he asked. "I did leave you my cell number when I first phoned you. Lily arrived two hours early—didn't that set off some kind of alarm bell?"

"She said you'd told her the wrong time."

"Does that seem likely? This arrangement won't work

out," he said before she could respond. "I'll find another instructor for Lily—one who can act responsibly."

His words stung. But Callie had no illusions about Lily Preston. The girl was trouble. And she certainly didn't want to have anything more to do with the man in front of her. Despite the fact her dormant libido had suddenly resurfaced and seemed to be singing, *pick me, pick me!*

She wanted to challenge him there and then to who was the responsible one—her for taking her eyes off Lily for a matter of minutes or him for clearly having little control over his daughter. But she didn't. *Think about the business. Think about the horses.* The last run-in she had with a parent had cost her nearly a quarter of her students and she was still struggling to recoup her losses. Three months earlier Callie had caught two students breaking the rules and had quickly cancelled all lessons with the troublesome sisters. But the girls' mother had other ideas, and she'd threatened to lodge a formal complaint with the Equestrian Federation. It could have led to the suspension of her instructor's license. Of course Callie could still teach without it, but her credentials were important to her. And she didn't want that kind of trouble again.

"That's your decision."

He didn't say another word. He just turned on his heels and walked away.

Callie slumped back against a fence post. Moments later she heard the rumble of an engine and didn't take a breath until the sound of tires crunching over gravel faded into nothing.

She looked at Indiana. She'd brought the horse with her from California—just Indy and three suitcases containing her most treasured belongings. Indiana had remained quarantined for some time after her arrival. Long enough for Callie to hunt through real estate lists until she'd found the perfect place to start her riding school.

Callie loved Sandhills Farm. Indiana and the rest of her nine horses were her life…her babies. *The only babies I'll have.* It made her think of *that man* and his four children.

A strange sensation uncurled in her chest, reminding her of an old pain—of old wishes and old regrets.

She took Indy's reins and led him toward the stables. Once he was back in the stall Callie headed for the office. She liked to call it an office, even though it essentially served as a tack room. She'd added a desk, a filing cabinet and a modest computer setup.

Joe, her part-time farmhand, had arrived and began the feeding schedule. Callie looked at her appointment book and struck Lily Preston's name off her daily list. There would be no Lily in her life…and no Lily's gorgeous father.

She looked around at her ego wall and at the framed photographs she'd hung up in no particular order. Pictures from her past, pictures of herself and Indiana at some of the events they'd competed in.

But not one of Craig.

Because she didn't want the inevitable inquisition. She didn't talk about Craig Baxter. Or her past. She'd moved halfway across the world to start her new life. Crystal Point had been an easy choice. Her father had been born in the nearby town of Bellandale and Callie remembered the many happy holidays she'd spent there when she was young. It made her feel connected to her Australian roots to make her home in the place where he'd been raised and lived until he was a young man. And although she missed California, this was home now. And she wasn't about to let that life be derailed by a gorgeous man with sexy green eyes. No chance.

Callie loved yard sales. Late Sunday morning, after her last student left, she snatched a few twenty dollar bills from her desk drawer and whistled Tessa to come to heel as she headed for her truck. The dog quickly leapt into the passenger seat.

The drive into Crystal Point took exactly six minutes. The small beachside community boasted a population of just eight hundred residents and sat at the mouth of the Bellan River, one of the most pristine waterways in the state. On the third Sunday of every month the small community hosted a "trunk and treasure" sale, where anyone who had something to sell could pull up their car, open the trunk and offer their wares to the dozens of potential buyers who rolled up.

The sale was in full swing and Callie parked a hundred yards up the road outside the local grocery store. She opened a window for Tessa then headed inside to grab a soda before she trawled for bargains. The bell dinged as she stepped across the threshold. The shop was small, but crammed with everything from fishing tackle to beach towels and grocery items. There was also an ATM and a pair of ancient fuel pumps outside that clearly hadn't pumped fuel for years.

"Good morning, Callie."

"Hi, Linda," she greeted the fifty-something woman behind the counter, who was hidden from view by a tall glass cabinet housing fried food, pre-packaged sandwiches and cheese-slathered hot dogs.

She picked out a soda and headed for the counter.

Linda smiled. "I hear you had a run-in with Noah Preston yesterday."

Noah? Was that his name? He'd probably told her when he'd made arrangements for his daughter's lessons, but Callie had appalling recall for names. *Noah.* Warmth pooled low in her belly. *I don't have any interest in that awful man.* And she wasn't about to admit she'd spent the past twenty-four hours thinking about him.

"Good news travels fast," she said and passed over a twenty dollar note.

Linda took the money and cranked the register. "In this place news is news. I only heard because my daughter volunteers as a guard at the surf beach."

Callie took the bait and her change. "The surf beach?"

"Well, Cameron was there. He told her all about it."

He did? "Who's Cameron?"

Linda tutted as though Callie should know exactly who he was. "Cameron Jakowski. He and Noah are best friends."

Callie couldn't imagine anyone wanting to be friends with Noah Preston.

"Cameron volunteers there, too," she said, and Callie listened, trying to not lose track of the conversation. "Noah used to, but he's too busy with all his kids now."

"So this Cameron told your daughter what happened?"

"Yep. He said you and Noah had an all-out brawl. Something to do with that eldest terror of his."

"It wasn't exactly a brawl," Callie explained. "More like a disagreement."

"I heard he thinks you should be shut down," Linda said odiously, her voice dropping an octave.

Callie's spine stiffened. Not again. When she'd caught the Trent sisters smoking in the stables, Sonya Trent had threatened the same thing. "What?"

"Mmm," Linda said. "And it only takes one thing to go wrong to ruin a business, believe me. One whiff of you being careless around the kids and you can kiss the place goodbye."

Callie felt like throwing up. Her business meant everything to her. Her horses, her home. "I didn't do anything," she protested.

Linda made a sympathetic face. "Of course you didn't, love. But I wouldn't blame you one bit if you had because of that little hellion." Linda sighed. "That girl's been nothing but trouble since her—"

The conversation stopped abruptly when the bell pealed

and a woman, dressed in a pair of jeans and a vivid orange gauze blouse, walked into the shop. Black hair curled wildly around her face and bright green eyes regarded Callie for a brief moment.

"Hello, Linda," she said and grabbed a bottle of water from one of the fridges.

"Evie, good to see you. Are you selling at the trunk sale today?" Linda asked.

Her dancing green eyes grew wide. "For sure," she said and paid her money. "My usual stuff. But if you hear of anyone wanting a big brass bed, let me know. I'm renovating one of the upstairs rooms and it needs to go. Catch you later."

She hurried from the shop and Linda turned her attention back to Callie.

"That's Evie Dunn," Linda explained. "She runs a bed and breakfast along the waterfront. You can't miss it. It's the big A-frame place with the monstrous Norfolk pines out the front. She's an artist and sells all kinds of crafting supplies, too. You should check it out."

Callie grimaced and then smiled. "I'm not really into handicrafts."

Linda's silvery brows shot up. "Noah Preston is her brother."

Of course. No wonder those green eyes had looked so familiar. Okay, maybe now she *was* a little interested. Callie grabbed her soda and left the shop. So, he wanted her shut down, did he?

She drove the truck in the car park and leashed Tessa. There were more than thirty cars and stalls set up, and the park was teeming with browsers and buyers. It took Callie about three minutes to find Evie Dunn. The pretty brunette had a small table laid out with craft wares and costume jewelry. She wandered past once and then navigated around for another look.

"Are you interested in scrapbooking?" Evie Dunn asked on her third walk by.

Callie stalled and eased Tessa to heel. She took a step toward the table and shrugged. "Not particularly."

Black brows rose sharply. "Are you interested in a big brass bed?"

Callie shook her head. "Ah, I don't think so."

Evie planted her hands on her hips. "Then I guess you must be interested in my brother?"

Callie almost hyperventilated. "What do you—"

"You're Callie, right?" The other woman asked and thrust out her hand. "I saw the name of your riding school on the side of your truck. I'm Evie. Lily told me all about you. You made quite an impression on my niece, which is not an easy feat. From what she told me, I'm certain she still wants you as her riding instructor."

There was no chance that was going to happen. "I don't think it's up to Lily."

"Made you mad, did he?"

Callie took a step forward and shook her hand. "You could say that."

Evie, whose face was an amazing mix of vivid color— green eyes and bright cherry lips—stared at her with a thoughtful expression that said she was being thoroughly summed up. "So, about the brass bed?" she asked and smiled. "Would you like to see it?"

Brass bed? Callie shook her head. Hadn't she already said she wasn't interested? "I don't think—"

"You'll love it," Evie insisted. "I can take you to look at it now if you like. Help me pack up and we can get going."

Callie began to protest and then stopped. She was pretty sure they weren't really talking about a bed. This was Noah

Preston's sister. And because he had quickly become enemy number one, if she had a lick of sense she'd find out everything she could about him and use it to her advantage. If Noah thought she would simply sit back and allow him to ruin her reputation, he could certainly think again. Sandhills Farm was her life. If he wanted a war, she'd give him one.

Previous text. And because he had quietly become the very
man she hated the very helpless she was hard to reach
him, she could about him because it's her very of any. If
he was trying to she would simply sit back and share. It didn't
make her say nothing respectably certain. Right again said the
dying was her life to be warned a way long to grant him cha

Chapter Two

Noah didn't know how to reach out to his angry daughter. He hurt for her. A deep, soul-wrenching hurt that transcended right through to his bones. But what could he do? Her sullen, uncommunicative moods were impossible to read. She skulked around the house with her eyes to the floor, hiding behind her makeup, saying little, determined to disassociate herself from the family he tried so frantically to keep together.

And she pined for the mother who'd abandoned her without a backward glance.

She'd deny it, of course. But Noah knew. It had been more than four years ago. Four and a half long years and they all needed to move on.

Yeah, right...like I've moved on?

He liked to think so. Perhaps not the way his parents or sisters thought he should have. But he'd managed to pull together the fractured pieces of the life his ex-wife discarded.

He had Preston Marine, the business his grandfather created and which he now ran, his kids, his family and friends. It was enough. More than enough.

Most of the time.

Except for the past twenty-four hours.

Because as much as he tried not to, he couldn't stop thinking about the extraordinarily beautiful Callie Jones and her glittering blue eyes. And the way she'd planted her hands on her hips. And the sinful way she'd filled out her jeans. For the first time in forever he felt a spark of attraction. More than a spark. It felt like a damned raging inferno, consuming him with its heat.

Noah stacked the dishes he'd washed and dried his hands, then checked his watch. He was due at Evie's around two o'clock; he'd promised her he'd help shift some furniture. Evie loved rearranging furniture.

Within ten minutes they were on their way. Hayley and Matthew, secured in their booster seats, chatted happily to each other while Jamie sat in the front beside Noah. His one-hundred-and-forty acre farm was only minutes out of Crystal Point and was still considered part of the small town. He'd bought the place a couple of years earlier, for a song of a price, from an elderly couple wanting to retire after farming sugar cane for close to fifty years. The cane was all but gone now, and Noah leased the land to a local farmer who ran cattle.

He dropped speed along The Parade, the long road separating the houses from the shore, and pulled up outside his sister's home. There was a truck parked across the road, a beat-up blue Ford that looked familiar. He hauled Hayley into his arms, grabbed Matty's hand and allowed Jamie to seize the knapsack from the backseat and then race on ahead. The kids loved Evie's garden, with its pond and stone paved walkways, which wound in tracks to a stone wishing well. And Noah kind of liked it, too.

"Look, Daddy...it's that dog," Jamie said excitedly, running toward a happy-looking pup tied to a railing near the front veranda.

The dog looked as familiar to him as the truck parked outside. His stomach did a stupid leap.

She's here? What connection did Callie Jones have to Evie? Before he could protest, Jamie was up the steps, opening the front door and calling his aunt's name.

Noah found them in the kitchen. Evie was cutting up pineapple and *she* was sitting at the long scrubbed table, cradling a mug in her hands. She looked up when he entered the room and smiled. A killer smile. A smile with enough kick to knock the breath from his chest. He wondered if she knew she had it, if she were aware how flawless her skin looked or how red and perfectly bowed her lips were. The hat was gone and her brown hair hung over one shoulder in a long braid.

Discomfort raced through him. Noah shifted Hayley on his hip and hung on tightly to Matty's hand. She looked him over, he looked her over. Something stirred, rumbling through his blood, taunting him a little.

Evie cleared her throat and broke the silence. "Well," she said. "How about I take the kids outside and you two can... talk?"

Noah didn't want to talk with her. He also knew he wouldn't be able to drag himself away.

Callie Jones had walked into his life. And he was screwed.

Callie couldn't speak. They were twins. *Twins.* Who looked to be about...four years old?

The same age as Ryan would have been...

She smiled—she wasn't sure how—and watched him hold the twins with delightful affection. He looked like Father of the Year. And he was, according to his sister. A single dad raising four children. A good man. The best.

A heavy feeling grew in her chest, filling her blood, sharpening her breath.

The children disappeared with Evie, and once they were alone she stood and flicked her braid down her back. He watched every movement, studying her with such open regard she couldn't stop a flush from rising over her skin.

I shouldn't want him to look at me like that.

Not this man who had quickly become the enemy.

"I didn't expect to see you…" he said, then paused. "So soon."

She inhaled deeply. "I guess you didn't. Frankly, I didn't *want* to see you."

His green eyes held her captive. "And yet you're here in my sister's house?"

Callie tilted her chin. "I'm looking at a bed."

The word *bed* quickly stirred up a whole lot of awareness between them. It was bad enough she thought the man was gorgeous—her blasted body had to keep reminding her of the fact!

"A bed?"

"Yes." Callie took another breath. Longer this time because she needed it. "You know, one of those things to sleep on."

That got him thinking. "I know what a bed is," he said quietly. "And what it's used for."

I'll just bet you do!

Callie turned red from her braid to her boots. "But now that I am here, perhaps you'd like to apologize?"

"For what?" He looked stunned.

For being a gorgeous jerk. "For being rude yesterday."

"Wait just a—"

"And for telling people my school should be closed down."

"What?"

"Are you denying it? I mean, you threatened me," she said, and as soon as the words left her mouth she felt ridiculous.

"I did what?"

She didn't miss the quiet, controlled tone in his voice. Maddeningly in control, she thought. Almost too controlled, as if he was purposefully holding himself together in some calm, collected way to prove he would not, and could not, be provoked.

"You said you'd see that I lost my license," she explained herself.

He looked at her. "And because of that you think I've been saying your school needs to be closed down?"

"Yes, I do."

"And who did you hear this from?"

Callie felt foolish then. Was she being paranoid listening to small-town gossip? *Have I jumped to conclusions?* When she didn't reply he spoke again.

"Local tongues, no doubt. I haven't said a word to anyone, despite my better judgment." He cocked a brow. "Perhaps you've pissed off someone else."

Retaliation burned on the end of her tongue. The infamous Callie Jones temper rose up like bile, strangling her throat. "You're such a jerk!"

He smiled. *Smiled.* As if he found her incredibly amusing. Callie longed to wipe the grin from his handsome face, to slap her hand across his smooth skin. To touch. To feel. And then, without explanation, something altered inside her. Something altered *between them.* In an unfathomable moment, everything changed.

He sees me...

She wasn't sure why she thought it. Why she felt it through to the blood pumping in her veins. But she experienced a strange tightening in her chest, constricting her breath, her movements. Callie didn't want anyone to see her. Not this man. Especially not this man. This stranger.

But he did. She was sure of it. *He sees that I'm a fraud. I can talk a tough line. But I live alone. I work alone. I am alone.*

And Noah Preston somehow knew it.

Bells rang in her head. Warning her, telling her to leave and break the incredible eye contact that shimmered like light between them.

"You need to keep a better handle on your daughter."

"I do?" he said, still smiling.

"She broke the rules," Callie said pointedly. "And as her parent, that's your fault, not mine."

"She broke the rules because you lacked good judgment," he replied.

Callie scowled, grabbed her keys and headed for the door. "Tell your sister thank you for the coffee."

He raised an eyebrow. "Did I hit a nerve?"

She rounded her shoulders back and turned around. "I'm well aware of my faults. I may not be all wisdom regarding the behavior of teenage girls, but I certainly know plenty about men who are arrogant bullies. You can point as much blame in my direction as you like—but that doesn't change the facts."

"I *did* hit a nerve."

"I wouldn't give you the satisfaction."

As she left the house and collected Tessa, Callie wasn't sure she took a breath until she drove off down The Parade.

Noah waited until the front door clicked shut and then inhaled deeply, filling his lungs with air. A jerk? Is that what he'd sounded like? He didn't like that one bit. A protective father, yes. But a jerk? He felt like chasing after her to set her straight.

Evie returned to the kitchen in record time, minus the kids. "They're watching a DVD," she said and refilled the kettle. Evie thought caffeine was a sure cure for anything. "So, that went well, did it?"

"Like a root canal."

"Ouch." She made a face. "She called you a jerk. And a bully."

"Eavesdropping, huh?"

She shrugged. "Only a bit. So, who won that battle in this war?" she asked, smiling.

He recognized his sister's look. "It's not exactly a war."

Evie raised a brow. "But you were mad at her, right?"

"Sure." He let out an impatient breath.

"Well." Evie stopped her task of making coffee. "You don't usually get mad at people."

Noah frowned. "Of course I do."

"No, you don't," Evie said. "Not even your pesky three sisters."

He shrugged. "Does this conversation have a point?"

"I was just wondering what she did to make you so...uptight?"

"I'm sure she told you what happened," Noah said, trying to look disinterested and failing.

Evie's eyes sparkled. "Well...yes, she did. But I want to hear it from you."

"Why?"

"So I can see if you get the same look on your face that she did."

"What look?" he asked stupidly.

Evie stopped what she was doing. A tiny smile curved her lips. "*That* look."

He shook his head. "You're imagining things."

Evie chuckled. "I don't think so. Anyway, I thought she was...nice."

Yeah, like a stick of dynamite. "You like everyone."

Evie laughed out loud. "Ha—you're not fooling me. You *like* her."

"I don't know her."

Noah dismissed his sister's suspicions. If he gave an inch, if he even slightly indicated he had thoughts of Callie Jones in any kind of romantic capacity, she'd be on the telephone to their mother and two other sisters within a heartbeat.

Romance...yeah, right. With four kids, a mortgage and a business to run—women weren't exactly lining up to take part in his complicated life.

He couldn't remember the last time he'd had a date. Eight months ago, he thought, vaguely remembering a quiet spoken, divorced mother of two who'd spent the entire evening complaining about her no-good, layabout ex. One date was all they'd had. He'd barely touched her hand. *I live like a monk.* That wasn't surprising, though—the fallout from his divorce would have sent any man running to the monastery.

Besides, he didn't want a hot-tempered, irresponsible woman in his life, did he? No matter how sexy she looked in her jeans. "So, where's this furniture you want me to move?" he asked, clapping his hands together as he stood.

Evie took the hint that the subject was closed. "One of the upstairs bedrooms," she said. "I want to paint the walls. I just need the armoire taken out into the hall."

"Oh, the antique cupboard that weighs a ton? Lucky me. At least this time I'm spared the stairs. Do you remember when Gordon and I first got the thing upstairs?"

Evie smiled, clearly reminiscing, thinking of the husband she'd lost ten years earlier. "And Cameron," she said. "You were all acting like a bunch of wusses that day, huffing and puffing over one little armoire."

Noah grunted as they took the stairs. "Damn thing's made of lead."

"Wuss," she teased.

They laughed some more and spent twenty minutes shifting the heaviest piece of furniture on the planet. When he was done, Noah wanted a cold drink and a back rub.

And that idea made him think of Callie Jones and her lovely blue eyes all over again.

"Feel like staying for dinner?" Evie asked once they were back downstairs. "Trevor's at a study group tonight," she said of her fifteen-year-old son.

"On a Sunday? The kid's keen."

"The kid's smart," Evie corrected. "He wants to be an engineer like his favorite uncle."

Noah smiled. "Not tonight, but thanks. I've gotta pick Lily up from the surf club at four. And it's a school day tomorrow."

Evie groaned. "God, we're a boring lot."

Noah wasn't going to argue with that. He grabbed the kids' things and rounded up the twins and Jamie. The kids hugged Evie and she waved them off from the front step.

"And don't forget the parents are back from their trip on Wednesday," she reminded him.

"I won't," he promised.

"And don't forget I'll need your help to move the armoire back into the bedroom in a few days. I'll call to remind you."

He smiled. "I won't forget."

"And don't forget to think about why you're refusing to admit that you're hot for a certain riding instructor."

Noah shook his head. "Goodbye, Evie."

She was still laughing minutes later when he drove off.

Noah headed straight for the surf club. Lily was outside when he pulled up, talking to Cameron. She scowled when she saw him and quickly got into the backseat, squeezing between the twins' booster seats. Normally, she would have resigned Jamie to the back. But not today. She was clearly still mad with him. Mad that *he'd* made it impossible for her to go back to Sandhills Farm, at least in her mind.

Noah got out of the pickup and turned his attention to his best friend. "So, Hot Tub, what have you been up to?"

Cameron half-punched him in the shoulder. "Would you stop calling me that?"

Noah grinned at his playboy friend and the unflattering nickname he'd coined years earlier.

"I'll do my best." He changed the subject. "Did Lily say anything to you about what happened yesterday?"

Cameron nodded. "You know Lily. I hear the horse lady's real cute."

Cute? That's not how Noah would describe Callie. Cute was a bland word meant for puppies and little girls with pink ribbons in their hair. Beautiful better described Callie Jones, and even that didn't seem to do her justice. Not textbook pretty, like Margaret, his ex, had been. Callie had a warm, rich kind of beauty. She looked like...the taste of a full-bodied Bordeaux. Or the scent of jasmine on a sultry summer's evening.

Get a grip. Noah coughed. "I have to get going."

Minutes later he was back on the road and heading home. By the time they reached the house Noah knew he wanted the truth from Lily. Callie Jones had called him a jerk. If he'd misjudged her like she said, he wanted to know. Lily tried her usual tactic of skipping straight to her bedroom, but he cut her off by the front door, just after the twins and Jamie had made it inside.

"Lily," he said quietly. "I want to talk to you."

She pulled her knapsack onto her shoulder and shrugged. "Don't you mean talk *at* me?"

He took a deep breath. "Did you ride that horse without permission yesterday?"

She rolled her eyes. "I told you what happened."

"Was it the truth?"

Lily shrugged. "Sort of." Her head shot up and she stared at him with eyes outlined in dark, smudgy makeup. "Is she blaming me?"

No, she's blaming me. And probably rightly so if the look on his daughter's face was anything to go by. Noah knew instantly that he'd overreacted. *Clearly. Stupidly.*

Noah suddenly felt like he'd been slapped over the back of the head. *I never overreact.* So, why her? Evie's words came back to haunt him.

You like her.

And he did. *She's beautiful, sassy and sexy as hellfire.*

But that wasn't really Callie Jones. It was an act—Noah knew it as surely as he breathed. How he knew he wasn't sure. Instinct maybe. Something about her reached him, drew him and made him want to *know* her.

Lily's eyes grew wider and suspicious. "You've seen her again, right?"

He wondered how she'd know that and thought it might be some fledgling female intuition kicking in. "Yes, I have."

She huffed, a childish sound that reminded him she was just thirteen. "Is she going to give me lessons?"

"I said we'd find you another instructor."

Lily's expression was hollow and she flicked her black hair from her eyes. "So, she won't?"

"I don't think so."

"Couldn't you ask her?"

Good question. He could ask her. Lily wanted her. Lily never wanted anything, never asked him for anything. But she wanted Callie Jones.

"Why is it so important to you to learn from Callie? There are other instructors in town."

She cast him a scowl. "Yeah, at the big training school

in town. It's full of rich stuck-ups with their push-button ponies."

"How do you know that?"

She chewed at her bottom lip for a moment and then said, "From school. The *Pony Girls* all go there."

Pony girls? Noah felt completely out of touch. "And?"

"The Trents," Lily explained. "Lisa and *Melanieeee*. They used to go to her school. *She* kicked them out a couple of months ago."

Melanie Trent. Lily's ex-best friend. And now her nemesis. "Why?"

"They were caught smoking in the stables," Lily supplied. "Big mistake. Anyway, I know that she lost some of her other students because of it. You know what the Trents are like. They don't like *anyone* telling them what to do."

Noah did know. Sonja Trent, the girls' mother, had worked reception for him a year earlier. He'd given her the post as a favor when her husband was laid off from his job at the local sugar mill. Two weeks later she left when Noah had made it clear he wasn't interested in having an affair with her. Sonja was married and unhappy—two good reasons to steer clear of any kind of involvement.

"Did you know *she* was some big-time rider?" Lily said, bringing Noah back to the present. "Like, I mean, really big time. Like she could have gone to the Olympics or something."

He tried not to think about the way his heart skipped a beat. "No, I didn't know that."

"If *she* teaches me then I'll be good at it, too. Better than *Melanie*. Way better. And maybe then she won't be so stuck-up and mean to Maddy all the time."

Maddy Spears was Lily's new/old best friend. Friends before Melanie had arrived on the scene and broken apart because Maddy was a quiet, sweet kid and not interested in flouting her parents' wishes by covering her face in make-up or wearing inappropriate clothes.

"I could apologize," Lily suggested and shrugged her bony shoulders.

That would be a first. Noah nodded slowly. "You could," he said, although he wasn't sure it would make any difference to the situation.

"I really want Callie, Dad," Lily said desperately.

You're not the only one. He cleared his throat. "I don't know, Lily…."

Noah wasn't sure how to feel about Lily's desperation to get lessons from Callie. Other than his sisters and mother, Lily hadn't let another woman into her life since Margaret had walked out.

Neither have I.

Lily didn't trust easily.

Neither do I.

"We'll see. Go and get washed up," he told her. "And maybe later you could help me with dinner?"

She grabbed the screen door and flung it open. "Maybe."

Her feet had barely crossed the threshold when Noah called her name. She stopped and pivoted on her Doc Martens. "What now?"

"Whoever you have lessons from, you have to follow the rules, okay?"

Her lips curled in a shadow of a smile. "Sure thing, Dad."

Noah watched his daughter sprint down the hall and disappear into her room with a resounding bang of the door. *Okay…now what?* But he knew what he had to do. He had to see Callie again. More to the point, he *wanted* to see her again. And he wondered if they made bigger fools than him.

Callie unhitched the tailgate and took most of the weight as it folded down. Indiana and Titan snorted restlessly, sensing the presence of other horses being unloaded and prepared for the Bellandale Horse Club show that day. Bellandale was a regional city of more than sixty thousand people and the event attracted competitors from many of the smaller surrounding townships.

Fiona Walsh, her friend and student, led both horses off the trailer, and Callie took the geldings in turn and hitched them to the side.

"I'm nervous," Fiona admitted as she ran her hands down her ivory riding breeches.

Callie unclipped Indiana's travel rug. "You'll be fine. This is your first competition—just enjoy the day. You and Titan have worked hard for this."

Fiona's carefully secured red hair didn't budge as she nodded enthusiastically. "Thanks for the pep talk. I'll go and get our stalls sorted."

Callie organized their gear once Fiona disappeared. Both horses were already groomed, braided and ready for tack, and by the time Fiona returned Callie had saddles and bridles adjusted and set. It took thirty minutes to find their allocated stalls, shovel in a layer of fresh sawdust, turn the horses into them and change into their jackets and long riding boots.

Callie's first event was third on the agenda and once she was dressed and had her competitors number pinned to her jacket she swung into the saddle and headed for the warm-up area. The show grounds were teaming with horses and riders and more spectators than usual, which she put down to the mild October weather. She warmed Indiana up with a few laps around the ring at a slow trot and then a collected canter. She worked through her transitions and practiced simple and flying changes. When she was done she walked Indy toward the main arena and waited for her name to be called.

The dressage test was a relatively simple one, but she gave it her full concentration. This was only her third show in as many months and she wanted to perform well. Indiana, as usual, displayed the skill and proficiency in his movements that had seen him revered by followers of the show circuit when she had been competing years before.

Before it all went wrong.

Before Craig Baxter.

Handsome, charming and successful and twelve years her senior, Craig had been a gifted rider. So gifted, in fact, that Callie often overlooked his moodiness and extreme perfectionism. Because underneath the charm and success, it had always only been about the competition. About results. About being the best.

And nearly four years after his death she still hurt.

It's better to have loved and lost...

Yeah…sure it was. Callie didn't believe that for one minute.

Love hurts. And it was off her agenda. Permanently.

What about sex? Is that off the agenda, too?

She'd thought so. But…in the last week she *had* been thinking about sex. Lots of sex. And all of it with Noah Preston. The kind of sex that had somehow invaded her normally G-rated life and made her have X-rated thoughts. Well, maybe not X-rated—she was still a little too homecoming queen for that. But certainly R-rated…

The announcement of her score startled her out of her erotic thoughts. She bowed her head to acknowledge the judges and left the dressage arena. As she cornered past three other riders waiting for their turn Callie eased Indiana to a halt. Because right there, in front of her, stood the object of all her recent fantasies.

Chapter Three

Dressed in jeans, a black chambray shirt and boots Noah looked so damned sexy it literally made her gasp. He held keys in one hand and a pair of sunglasses in the other.

She stared at him, determined to hold his gaze. Finally, curiosity got the better of her and she clicked Indiana forward. "What do you want?"

He moved toward her and touched Indy's neck. "Nice-looking horse."

"Thank you," she said stiffly, hoping he couldn't see the color rising over her cheeks. Callie collected the reins and swung herself out of the saddle. "Did you want something?" she asked again once both feet were planted on the ground.

"I did."

So tell me what it is and go away so I can stop thinking about how totally gorgeous you are and how much you make me think about wanting all the things I never thought I'd want again.

"How did you know I was here?"

"Your apprentice told me where to find you."

Joe? Callie wanted to ring his neck. "So you've found me. And?"

"I'd like to talk to you."

Callie tilted her chin. "What have I done now?" she asked, clutching the reins tightly so he wouldn't notice her hands were shaking.

He half smiled and Callie's stomach did a silly leap. "I guess I deserve that," he said.

She moved Indiana forward. She wouldn't fall for any lines, no matter how nicely he said them. She wouldn't be tempted to feel again. She couldn't. It hurt too much. "Oh, I see—today you come in peace?"

"I wanted to apologize."

"You're a week too late," she said stiffly and led the horse away. Callie felt him behind her as she walked—felt his eyes looking her over as he followed her past the rows of small stables until she reached their allocated stall.

Fiona came out from the adjoining stall. "Hi, Noah," Fiona greeted with a cheek-splitting grin. Callie didn't miss how the other woman's hand fleetingly touched his arm.

Clearly, no introductions were required. Fiona saw her look and explained that she taught his son at the local primary school and took an art class with his sister, Evie.

"So you two know each other?" Fiona asked.

"Yes," he replied. "We do."

"I'd better go," Fiona said quickly and began leading Titan from his stall. "My event is up next. Wish me luck."

Callie watched her friend lead the big chestnut gelding away and then turned her attention to the man in front of her.

"Okay," she said. "You can apologize now."

He laughed and the rich, warm sound dipped her stomach

like a rolling wave. Callie felt like smiling, but she wouldn't. She *wanted* to be mad at him—it made her feel safe.

"I overreacted last week," he said. "I know Lily took your horse without permission."

Her chin came up. "Bravo. I'll bet saying that was like chewing glass," she said as she opened the stall and ushered Indiana inside. Then she clicked the bottom door in place. "So," she said, "was there something else you wanted to discuss?"

"First, that you reconsider and give Lily riding lessons."

Callie didn't try to disguise her astonishment. "I thought you were going to find her another instructor."

"Apparently you're the best around."

"Yes," she replied, fighting the rapid thump of her heart. He was close now. Too close. "I am."

"And I want the best for my daughter."

"You should have thought about that before you called me an irresponsible nutcase."

His green eyes looked her over. "Is that what I said?"

Callie unbuttoned her jacket. "Words to that effect," she said, feeling suddenly hot and sweaty in the fine-gauge wool coat she'd had tailored to fit like a glove. She longed to strip off her hat, but the idea of him seeing the very unattractive hairnet she wore to keep her thick hair secure under the helmet stopped her.

He smiled. "Then I owe you an apology for that, as well."

"Yes, you do. So, anything else?"

"That you give me another chance," he said quietly. "I might be a jerk on occasion…but I'm not such a bad guy."

She snorted and that made him smile again. God, her hormones were running riot. Did this man know how earth-shatteringly gorgeous he was? She had to pull herself together. He leaned back against the stall and Callie watched, suddenly mesmerized as the cotton shirt stretched across his chest as he moved. *One step and I could touch him. One tiny step and I could place my hands over his broad shoulders.*

"So, do we have an arrangement?"

His voice jerked her thoughts back. "No, we don't."

"Are you going to play hard to get?"

The double meaning of his words could not be denied and Callie blushed wildly. She looked at her feet, thinking that any minute she was going to plant one of her size nines into her mouth and say something she'd regret. And typically, she did exactly that.

"I'm not playing anything with you," she said hotly. "As you pointed out so clearly last weekend, I don't have the skills required to handle your daughter. What I do have is a business to run...a business that means everything to me. I work hard and I won't do anything that could tarnish my reputation."

His gaze narrowed. "And you think teaching Lily would?"

"I think..." She stopped. It wasn't about Lily. It was about him. She only hoped he didn't realize it. "I think...another teacher would be better for her. Someone she would actually listen to."

"And if I promised that she would listen to you, Callie?"

She drew in a breath. It was the first time he'd said her name. It sounded personal. Intimate almost. "You can't promise something like that."

"She'll do what I ask."

Yeah...like putty in his hands. That's how Callie felt at the moment. "Look," she said pointedly. "All I want to do is run my school and care for my horses and try to fix up my house, which is crumbling around my ears. I just don't want any drama."

It sounded lame. Callie knew it. *He* knew it.

Something passed between them. Awareness? Recognition? A look between two people who hardly knew one another…and yet, strangely, on some primal level, had a deep connection. More than merely man to woman. More…*everything.* It scared the breath out of her. Thinking about him was one thing. *Feeling* something for him was another altogether.

"And there's nothing I can offer you that might make you change your mind?"

Callie's temperature rose and launched off her usual, well-controlled sensible-gauge. It was ridiculous. She couldn't imagine everything he said to her had some kind of sexual innuendo attached to it.

"Nothing."

"Even though you say you need the cash?"

It sounded foolish put like that. But she wasn't going to give in. "Exactly."

"That doesn't make a lot of sense."

"Well, you know me—all bad judgment and recklessness." She picked up the pitch fork. "Now, if you don't mind, I have to go and watch Fiona."

He half shrugged, looked at the pitch fork as though she might consider running him through with it, then took a small card from his pocket and passed it to her. "If you change your mind—"

"I won't." Callie folded the small business card between her fingers and opened the door to Indiana's stall. She slipped inside and waited a full five minutes before emerging—and only when she was certain Noah Preston had left.

Noah usually let the kids stay up a little later on Saturday nights. But by eight-thirty the twins were falling asleep on the sofa and Jamie took himself off to bed just after Hayley and Matthew were tucked beneath the covers.

Lily, however, decided to loiter in the kitchen, flicking through cupboards as she complained about the lack of potato chips. She made do with an opened box of salted crackers.

"So," she said as she sat. "Did you ask her?"

Noah stopped packing the dishwasher and looked at his daughter. The makeup and piercings and black clothes seemed more out of place than usual in the ordinariness of the timber kitchen. He wished she'd ditch the gothic act, but he'd learned fast that barking out ultimatums only fueled her rebelliousness.

"Yes."

Lily looked hopeful and Noah's heart sank. How did he tell his kid the truth? "She's thinking about it," he said, stretching the facts.

His daughter's expression changed quickly. "She's still mad at me?" Lily dropped the box of crackers and stood. "She's the best, Dad. And learning from the best is important. It means I might get to be the best at something, too."

She looked painfully disappointed and Noah felt every ounce of her frustration. If she'd followed Callie's rules, it wouldn't have been a problem.

"Lily, whoever you get lessons from, you'll have to follow the rules."

Lily's dramatic brows rose. "I'm not the one who shouted at her."

Noah stiffened. "I didn't shout. We had a conversation."

"Yeah, and after that she said she wouldn't teach me."

He had to admit his daughter had a point. If he hadn't acted so irrationally and lost his cool with Callie, he figured Lily would have been able to stay at the school. Lily had messed up, but so had *he*.

"'Night, Dad," she said unhappily and left the room.

Noah looked at the clock. He was weary but not tired. He left the dishwasher and headed for the living room. The big sofa welcomed him as he sat and grabbed the remote.

Another long Saturday night loomed ahead. He flicked

channels absently and settled for a movie he'd seen before. It didn't hold his attention for long. He kept thinking of Callie. She was a real dynamo. All feisty and argumentative, high octane. But underneath, he saw something else…something more. He wasn't sure how he knew—but he did. Whatever was going on with her, she wore it like a suit of armor. And he was interested in knowing what lay underneath all that fire and spirit. Hell, he was more than interested. Way more. The way she'd glared at him from beneath her hat, the way she'd filled out her riding jodhpurs… His skin burned thinking about it.

He flicked channels again, but it was no use. Television wouldn't hold his attention tonight. More so than usual, he felt alone and…lonely. Absurd when he lived in a house filled with children. And when he considered how great his family was. He loved his kids. His parents were exceptional, and his sisters were the best he could ask for.

But right now he wanted more than that. He needed more than that.

But what?

Company? Someone to talk with?

Sex?

Perhaps it was more about sex than he was prepared to admit. Up until a week ago he'd been in a kind of sexual hibernation. But Callie had him thinking about it. And got him hard *just* thinking about it. And not the vague, almost indistinct inclination that usually stirred him. This was different. Way different.

Maybe I should ask her out?

That was crazy. That would be like standing in front of a bulldozer.

She can't stand you, he reminded himself. *Okay, maybe I'll just ask her to reconsider about Lily again?*

Despite his brain telling him to forget the idea, Noah

picked up the telephone and dialed the number he couldn't recall memorizing but somehow had. She answered on the fourth ring.

"Callie, it's Noah Preston."

Silence screeched like static. Finally she spoke. "Oh—hello."

"Sorry to call so late."

A pause. "That's okay—I'm not in bed yet."

His body tightened. He had a startling image in his head and shook himself. *Maybe I will ask her out.* "I was wondering if you—"

"I haven't reconsidered," she said, cutting him off.

"What?"

"About Lily," she said on a soft breath.

All he could think about was that same breath against his skin. "I was actually—"

"Janelle Evans," she said quickly, cutting him off again.

Noah paused. "What?" he asked again.

"She's an instructor just out of town. She has a good reputation. She breeds quarter horses. I have her number if you're interested."

Oh, I'm interested all right. But not in Janelle Evans.

She was talking fast and Noah knew she was eager to end the call. *Bulldozer,* he reminded himself. "Ah—sure."

He took the number she rattled off and had to ask her to repeat the last few digits because she spoke so quickly.

"Well—goodbye."

He hesitated, feeling the sting of her reluctance to engage in conversation. "Yeah, okay—goodbye."

She hung up and he dropped the telephone on the sofa. He needed a shower—as cold as he could stand. Then he'd go to bed and sleep off the idea that he wanted to make love to Callie Jones more than he'd wanted to do anything for a long time.

* * *

On Sunday morning Callie woke at seven, after spending a restless night fighting with the bedsheets.

It was all Noah Preston's fault. She didn't ask for his late-night call. She didn't want to hear his sexy voice just before she went to bed. She didn't want to spend the night thinking about him.

She dressed and made short work of a bowl of cereal topped with fruit, then grabbed her hat and headed outside. The sun was up, already warming the early October morning air. She fed Tessa then headed for the stables, where Joe waited outside Indiana's stall.

"Are you taking the big fella out this morning?"

Callie shook her head. "Not today." Indy's long head swung over the top of the door and she ran her hands down his face. "'Morning, my darling boy." She turned back to Joe. "He did well yesterday, two firsts and a third, so he gets a day off. Give him a feed, will you, and then tack up Kirra. The English saddle please."

Joe made a face. "What do I tell the kid?"

Callie frowned. "What kid?"

"The one who's here for a lesson."

Callie shook her head. "I don't have anyone booked until eleven."

"I know," Joe said. "I checked the booking sheet. But she's here." Joe pointed to the office. "I put her in there," he said, then more seriously, "and told her not to touch anything."

Callie strode the twenty meters to the office and swung the half-opened door back on its hinges. She stood in the threshold and looked at the young girl sitting at her desk.

"What are you doing here?"

Lily Preston swiveled in the chair and got to her feet. "Um…I'm here for my lesson."

Callie inhaled deeply. "You're not having a lesson."

"But I thought—"

Callie placed her hands on her hips. "You have to go home, Lily." She turned on her heels and went to walk away but stopped when the teenager spoke.

"Please."

She turned back and looked at the teenager, whose green eyes were wide open, their expression sincere. Lily *was* sorry. Callie could feel it. Something tugged at her heartstrings.

Callie took a deep breath. "Indiana is my horse, Lily. And as quiet as he is, you could have been badly hurt. And I would have been responsible."

Lily's chin lifted, half defiant. "But I can ride a bit."

"A bit isn't good enough for a horse like Indiana, especially in an ill-fitting bridle and without a saddle."

Lily looked shame-faced beneath her makeup. "I really didn't mean to cause any trouble," she said. "I just…sometimes I just *do* things. I don't know why. I do things I know are stupid, but I can't help myself."

The tug on Callie's heart grew stronger. She knew exactly what Lily meant. Kindred spirits, she thought. But, oh, God…what should she do? Say yes to this girl who looked at her with such raw intensity. A girl, she suspected, who rarely showed that side of herself to anyone. But a girl whose father she couldn't stop thinking about. Who, without even trying, was making Callie feel, imagine.

"I'll do whatever you want," Lily said quickly, almost desperately. "Please teach me."

Before Callie could reply Joe stuck his head around the door to tell her Kirra was ready. She thanked him, then returned her attention to the teenager. "I'll tell you what—you stay out of trouble while I work my horse and we'll talk after." She stood aside for Lily to pass. "No promises, just talk."

Callie led Lily from the stables and told her to stay put

near the dressage arena. She gave her an old soda crate to sit on and then took the red bay mare into the arena. She worked her for twenty minutes, trying to concentrate on the maneuvers and transitions from trot to canter. But her mind wasn't really on the job. Lily sat on the sidelines, watching her, masked behind her makeup.

Ten minutes later Noah Preston's silver utility vehicle pulled up outside the stables. Callie continued with her ride, watching as he got out and opened the back door of the truck. The children stepped out. The older boy grabbed the hands of the twins and listened as his father spoke to them. Then he headed for Lily. He had a great walk, she thought. And he looked so good in jeans and a black T-shirt. Way too good.

Callie watched as the kids followed behind him. And again it stirred something inside her. An old longing. And it gave her a snapshot of a life she'd never have.

Ryan...

The longing turned into a pain—a piercing, incredible hurt that always took root behind her ribs when she thought about the beautiful baby boy she'd lost when he was just two days old.

I miss you Ryan...I miss holding you...I miss watching you grow up and become the person you could have been.

Kirra sensed her distraction and started prancing sideways at a trot. Callie got her quickly under control and eased her to a halt in the center of the arena. And she watched as Noah began talking with his daughter. Lily nodded, he shook his head. Lily said something, he replied. The conversation lasted for some minutes and the three younger Preston children stood quietly behind their father. Finally, Lily waved her arms about and stomped off toward the truck. He said something to the three kids and they sat on the soda crate. Then he headed through the gate and into the arena.

Callie dismounted and pulled the reins over Kirra's head,

collecting them in her left hand. She fought the ridiculous impulse to take off her safety hat and smooth out her hair or rub her hands down her breeches.

He stopped about two feet in front of her. "Hello," he said.

Callie swallowed. "Hi."

He went to say something but then stopped. He patted the horse instead. He had nice hands, she noticed. Tanned and strong looking. She quickly snapped herself out of her silly female fantasy. "I was going to call you," she said. "You beat me to it."

"I knew she'd be here."

"You did? How?"

"Because you were the last thing we talked about last night. And I know Lily—when she gets her mind stuck on something, she can be impossible to deal with."

Callie raised her brows. "Looks like you're surrounded by impossible women."

My God, am I flirting? That's what it sounds like.

And he smiled. As though he liked it. "I could think of worse things."

Everything around her suddenly felt hot—the air in her lungs, the sand beneath her boots. "Anyway—she didn't do any harm while she was here."

"She's changed since her mother left."

Not what he wanted to say, Callie was sure of it. It was too familiar, too personal, too everything. And Callie wanted to clamp her hands over her ears. She didn't want to hear any more. She didn't want to know him. She didn't want to know *more* of him.

"No problem." It was a pitiful attempt at sounding indifferent.

"She used to be…sweet. A real sweet kid. And then she changed almost overnight."

Callie felt another surge of feeling for Lily. She knew all

about change. She knew what grief and hurt could do to a person. "Is that the reason for the makeup and black clothes?"

He shrugged. "Something to hide behind, I guess. She still wants riding lessons."

Callie clicked Kirra forward and began to walk from the arena. "Well, Janelle Evans is a good instructor."

He stepped in beside her. "She's asked for you."

"She can't...you can't...I just..."

Something happened then. Her legs stopped moving. Her lungs stopped breathing as she turned and their eyes locked. For one extraordinary moment Callie knew that whatever she was feeling, he was feeling it, too. It was crazy, heady and blindingly powerful.

He spoke first. "Lily rarely asks for anything."

Callie continued walking. "Which means?"

"Which means I'm inclined to do whatever I can to see that she gets what she wants."

They got to the gate. Callie tied Kirra to the railing, took a deep breath. "I'm not sure I—"

"Callie," he said "Please, reconsider." He placed his hand on her arm. A light touch, but the electricity coursing between their skin could not be denied. He looked at his hand but didn't remove it. Callie stood still, held in place by his touch, by the mere wisp of space that lay between them. "Lily needs you." He paused, watching her. "And I...and I need you."

Chapter Four

Callie moved her arm. Away from his touch. Away from temptation. Away from the realization that she liked how his hand felt against her skin.

I need you...

There was something startlingly intimate about the way he spoke the words. She couldn't remember the last time a man had said that to her. Maybe never. Craig hadn't needed her. And Noah Preston didn't need her, either...not really. He just wanted her to teach his daughter to ride a horse.

"I can't."

He smiled. "Yes, you can."

God, he was relentless. Callie lifted her chin. "I said I can't."

"She'll be on her best behavior," he said.

Callie expelled a heavy breath. "Even if she is, I'm not—"

"Is your unwillingness actually about Lily?" he interrupted her. "Or something else?"

Her heart quickened. "Like what?"

He looked at her. Really looked. Callie felt compelled to turn her gaze away, but she didn't. *Couldn't.* She'd never felt this kind of intensity with anyone before. She'd spent years convincing herself she didn't want it.

"I thought that perhaps you and..." He stopped, hesitated and sort of half smiled. "I think we...I think *we* might have started off on the wrong foot."

He wasn't kidding. But she wasn't about to admit it. She wasn't about to admit to anything. Instead, she thought about the practical. "Why this sudden confidence in my abilities?"

"Because Lily believes in you."

Callie didn't break their eye contact. "Even though you don't?"

"And if I said I did? Would you reconsider teaching Lily? If I apologized again for being a jerk and asked you to do this for my daughter?"

Her insides quivered. *Don't be nice to me.* "You don't give up easily."

He shook his head. "Not when I want something." He looked around. "I heard you'd lost some students recently."

She stared at him. "How did you know that?"

He grinned. "Local gossip."

Callie's skin prickled. Just like the local gossip she'd listened to last weekend. "Yes, I did."

He looked around, to the house, then back to her. "So, it looks like you're not doing well financially."

More prickles. "I'm not filing for bankruptcy just yet."

A full smile this time. "I didn't mean to imply you were," he said carefully. "But I thought perhaps we could strike a deal."

Cautious, Callie's interest spiked. "What kind of deal?"

"Your usual fee—plus I'll help prevent your house from 'crumbling around your ears.'"

She stilled. "And how exactly will you do that?"

"I'll do whatever maintenance needs to be done while Lily's having her lessons."

Callie looked at him suspiciously. "Do you work construction?"

"No," he replied. "But I know my way around a toolbox."

I'll bet you do. Suddenly she was tempted. Very tempted. She *did* need the money. And as for his offer to help repair her house…that idea dangled like a juicy carrot in front of her nose. With windows that wouldn't open, doors needing repair, fence palings hanging loose and the knowledge she needed to chase the entire house with a paintbrush, the lure of his offer teased her. Refusing would be impulsive. And foolish.

And Lily…she wanted to help Lily. Helping Lily was suddenly important to her.

Oh, hell.

"Okay," she said quickly, before she had time to think about what it might mean to have him hanging around her house every Sunday morning. Him and his adorable kids.

Noah looked instantly pleased. "Good. Will you start today?"

She shook her head. "No. Next week. Sunday, nine o'clock."

He stepped back, finally, and she dipped underneath Kirra's neck, feeling safer with the horse between them. "Thank you, Callie. You won't regret it."

Too late…she already did.

He walked off without another word, collecting his kids along the way. Once his truck had disappeared down the driveway, Callie took off Kirra's tack and led her to the washing bay.

Joe appeared, his hair spotted with straw from the bales he'd been lugging off the truck and into the feed room.

"So, what's the deal with Vampira?" he asked, grimacing as he passed Callie an old towel. "Scary." He shuddered. "Do you reckon she's got tattoos, as well?"

Callie wasn't about to admit that she had one herself. "That's not nice."

He shrugged his lanky shoulders. "If my little sister went around looking like that my parents would go ballistic." He made a disagreeable face. "Was that her dad—Noah Preston?"

Callie stopped rubbing the towel over Kirra's flanks. "Do you know him?"

"I met him last weekend when he was looking for you. My Uncle Frank bought one of his boats last year."

Her interest increased tenfold. "He sells boats?"

Joe shook his head. "He designs boats," he replied. "And builds them. Top-of-the-range stuff. He's got a big factory in town. Uncle Frank reckons his boats are the best around."

Noah was a boat builder. And a single dad. And too gorgeous for her peace of mind.

As she led Kirra back to her stall, Callie couldn't stop thinking about how deeply he affected her. And how much she wished he didn't.

The Crystal Point Twilight Fair was an annual event that raised funds for the local elementary school and volunteer Rural Fire Brigade. Callie had been invited to provide horse rides for a small fee. The money collected would go directly back to the organizing committee, but it gave her an opportunity to promote her riding school. Sunshine and Peanuts, her two quietest geldings, loved the attention and happily walked around the makeshift yard she'd put together with a little help from Joe. There was also a jumping castle, a small carousel, a baby animal pen and a variety of stalls selling homemade cakes and candies and assorted handicrafts.

"So, are you staying for the dance later?" Fiona asked as she navigated Peanuts past her.

Callie checked the child clinging to Sunshine's saddle and smiled at her friend as they passed one another. "In this outfit?" she said, motioning a hand gesture to her worn jeans, thin sweater and riding boots. "I'll skip it. I have to get the horses back anyhow."

On their next passing Fiona spoke again. "I could use the company."

"Maybe another time.'

Callie didn't socialize much. Or at all. There seemed to be little time in her life for anything other than work. And she wasn't exactly in the right frame of mind to be thinking about dating.

Dating? Where did that come from?

She maneuvered the pony toward the entrance and helped the child dismount. The queue had grown and about six kids were waiting in line. She took the next one in turn.

An older woman came forward with two small children. They looked familiar and she glanced at the woman, taking in her attractive features, dark hair and deep green eyes.

Noah's children.

Callie's breath caught in her throat. The blond-haired pair were unmistakable. They were Noah's twins. And she was certain the striking-looking older woman was his mother.

"Is something wrong?" the woman asked.

Callie shook her head. "Of course not… It's just that I know your…Evie," she said quietly, suddenly self-conscious. "And Lily," she explained. "I'll be teaching Lily."

The other woman smiled. "Yes, I know. My son told me."

Callie's skin heated. She stopped herself from looking around to see if he was close by. "Let's get the kids up on the pony."

"Can they go together?"

"Yes." Callie took the little girl's hand and helped her into the saddle. She was such a pretty child and had an adorable smile. Something uncurled inside her with a sharp, ripping intensity. She'd become so adept at covering her feelings that children didn't normally do this to her...didn't make her think about Ryan. But this little girl did. With her bright eyes and rosy cheeks, Noah's daughter made her remember all she had lost.

Callie managed a smile, fought against the lump suddenly forming in her throat and helped the little boy aboard the pony. He was quieter than his sister and didn't say a word, while the little girl chatted for the entire duration of the pony ride.

She walked the perimeter of the arena a few times and learned that the girl's name was Hayley and her brother was Matthew. They were four and a half and couldn't wait to start school soon. They loved their grandma and Aunt Evie and didn't like green vegetables all that much.

By the time the ride was over Callie had a strange pain wedged behind her rib cage.

She headed for the gate, passing Fiona on another round, and was surprised to find the children's grandmother gone.

And Noah stood in her place.

"Daddy!" Hayley exclaimed. "Look at me."

He was smiling that mega-watt smile and Callie's stomach rolled over. "Hello."

She swallowed hard and tried not to think about how good he looked in jeans and a navy golf shirt. "Hi." She glanced into his eyes, saw awareness, felt that familiar jolt of attraction. "Your mother?"

He nodded. "She's gone back to trawling the craft stalls." He gestured to the kids. "Did they behave themselves?"

"They were perfect little angels."

He laughed out loud. "Angels? That doesn't sound like my kids."

Callie smiled back. "She's a natural. So is Matthew."

Both children looked pleased as could be with the praise. He hauled Hayley into his arms and then placed her onto the ground. Matthew followed soon after. The kids moved around to the front of Sunshine and began stroking his nose.

"So, can you take a break from this gig?"

"A break?" she echoed. "What for?"

He smiled. "To talk. You could let me buy you a soda."

"I really don't think—"

"I'd like to get to know you better."

There it was, right out in the open. "Why—"

"You know why, Callie."

Without anything to hide behind, Callie felt so raw, so completely exposed, she could barely draw breath. She stared at him for a moment and then looked toward the now queue of one waiting for a turn on a pony. "Um…I probably shouldn't," she said on a whisper. "There's someone still—"

"We'll wait."

We'll wait. Him and the children she wanted so desperately to avoid—but somehow couldn't.

Fiona chose that moment to come up behind her and announced she'd happily take charge of the remaining child and then volunteered Joe to help with Sunshine. Before she had a chance to protest, Joe had taken the gelding and Callie found herself leaving the arena with Noah and his children.

"That was fun, Daddy," Hayley said excitedly.

"Was it, poppet?" He looked at Callie as they walked. "Maybe the twins could have riding lessons, too."

"Maybe," Callie replied and almost jumped from her skin when Hayley grasped her hand. She stopped walking immediately and looked down. The little girl tugged her forward, giggled and acted as though holding her hand was the most natural thing in the world.

Instinct kicked in and she went to pull her hand away... but something stopped her. Maybe it was the lovely, infectious laugh coming from the little girl. Or perhaps it was that Noah was watching her with such blistering intensity she knew that if she moved, if she rejected the child's hand, he'd see it. And he'd see more than that. He'd see through her and into the parts of herself she kept so fiercely guarded.

"Anything wrong, Callie?"

Already suspicious, she thought. Already figuring her out. "Not a thing," she lied and allowed herself to be led toward a refreshments stall.

He bought drinks all round and Callie had just cranked the cap off her soda when Hayley announced she wanted her face painted.

"Can we, Daddy, please?" she pleaded and skipped toward the face-painting tent.

He nodded and they all followed. He passed the colorfully decorated painter a couple of notes from his wallet. Hayley insisted on going first while Matthew waited patiently behind his more flamboyant sister.

Callie stood to the side. "Where's your other son?" she asked. "And Lily?"

"Jamie's with Evie. And Lily doesn't do fairs."

Callie half smiled. "Too cool, huh?"

"Or stubborn."

"She's headstrong," Callie said. "And there's nothing wrong with that."

He crossed his arms and she couldn't help looking at his chest. He was remarkably fit and broad shouldered and her awareness of him spiked. It had been eons since she'd been this attracted to someone. Maybe never. She'd been with Craig for so many years, and any true desire they'd felt for one another had faded long before his death. But Noah had kickstarted her libido with a resounding thud.

"Speaking from experience?" he asked quietly while keeping a watch on his kids.

Callie got her feelings back on track. "I'm sure my parents thought me willful. I liked to do things my own way."

"And still do, I imagine."

She wasn't about to deny it. "She'll come around," Callie assured him, sensing it was true, although she had no idea why she thought so. "Raising a teenage girl wouldn't be easy—especially alone."

"Sometimes...no. But they're all pretty well behaved most of the time. Even Lily."

"Do they see their mother much?" she asked before she could stop herself. She wondered why on earth she was so interested in this man and his children. She wasn't usually so inquisitive. Who was she kidding? She was *never* inquisitive.

"No," he replied. "They don't."

Callie's tongue tingled with another question, but she held back. The more she knew about him, the more *he'd* want to know about her...and she wasn't ready for that. She wasn't sure she ever would be. But despite her reticence, she suddenly had the image of his four motherless children burned deep in her heart.

Heaven help me...I'm actually in danger of falling for this man.

Noah felt her pain. She'd done a great job of building a big wall around whatever it was that haunted the depths of her blue eyes. *But not quite good enough.*

"Will I see you tonight?" he asked, determined to keep her talking.

"For the dance?" She shook her head. "No. I have to take the horses back home."

He pressed on. "You could come later."

She stepped back. "I don't…I don't…it's just that I don't…"

"You don't what?" he asked, picking up her trailing words.

"I don't date," she said bluntly.

Noah half smiled. So they had something in common. "Neither do I," he admitted and when she looked surprised, he explained what he meant. "Four kids make dating… difficult." He raised his brows. "What's your excuse?"

She shrugged and took a deep breath. "I don't have one."

Not exactly the truth and they both knew it. "Are you nursing a broken heart?"

She crossed her arms and dangled the soda bottle between her fingertips. "Not the kind you might be imagining," she said softly.

Noah's curiosity soared. He wanted to know all about her. Everything. She'd been hurt in the past, that much was obvious. But by whom? "Want to talk about it?"

She shook her head again and stepped back fractionally, as if she was looking for an escape. "I should go." She tapped the soda bottle. "Thank you for the drink."

She said goodbye to the kids and walked away, leaving him staring after her.

Callie sat on the edge of her bed and examined the contents of her open wardrobe.

She'd arrived home an hour earlier. The horses were fed, the dog was asleep in the kitchen and she was left wondering why she was actually considering dressing up and heading back to the fair. But Fiona had called and begged her to go. So, her friend needed her. That was as good a reason as any. It wasn't because there was a band playing and that there would be dancing. It wasn't because Noah would be there.

She knew getting involved with him was out of the question.

He has four children.

He had what she would never have. Her heart felt so heavy in her chest when she thought about it. She'd kept a lid on her feelings for more than four years and had accepted she could never have another child because of complications during Ryan's birth. Ryan was her child…and he was gone. But in a matter of days, and without warning, the lid had lifted off and suddenly she was *all* feelings…*all* memory…*all* want.

Noah makes me want.

Desiring him was one thing. She hadn't expected to *like* him. She hadn't expected to like anyone ever again.

Forty minutes later she'd dressed and drove back to the fair.

It was well past eight o'clock by the time she arrived. The stalls and kiddie games had been replaced by a large dance floor and clusters of tables and chairs. The whole scene had been decorated with hundreds of tiny lights, and food and drink vendors were on hand to satisfy appetites. The turnout was impressive. People had dressed up and were clearly enjoying themselves. The band was good and the dance floor was busy. Callie spotted Fiona standing near a tent where drinks were being served and quickly headed for her friend.

"You're here!" Fiona squealed and hugged her close. "Thank goodness."

"You said you could use the company."

"I could. Great dress—aren't you glad I insisted you buy it?"

It *was* a great dress—a flimsy chiffon concoction of muted caramel shades with a halter top. The skirt fell just above her knees. "Of course."

"Fiona!"

They both turned at the sound of the pleasantly pitched female voice. A dark haired woman with the most amazing green eyes came toward them, buffering against a few people in her stride.

"M.J.," Fiona greeted. "Good to see you."

Fiona introduced them and the green-eyed beauty made a startled sound. "*You're* Callie? Lily's riding instructor?"

Callie bristled. "You know Lily?"

M.J. laughed delightfully. "She's my niece," she explained. "I'm Noah's sister."

Of course. The resemblance to Evie was unmistakable. And those eyes were all Preston. "I didn't realize he had more than one."

"There are three of us girls."

"Is Evie here?" she asked, acutely conscious that Noah would be nearby.

I'm not here for him. I'm not. I can't be.

"Nah—she's looking after the kids," M.J. said. "It's just me and Noah tonight."

And then, as if drawn by some inexplicable force, Callie turned her neck and met his gaze head-on.

Noah knew the exact moment Callie arrived. It was as if some internal radar, attuned to only her, had taken hold of him. The area seemed smaller, the air heavy, and the noise of glasses clinking and people speaking faded into a barely audible sound. She looked incredible. The dress, the hair tumbling down her back, the heels that showed off her amazing legs—he wondered if any of the half a dozen people around him heard the strangled sound that formed in his throat. She must have felt him staring at her because she turned her head and looked right at him.

A blinding and electrical visual contact hit him from his

feet to his fingertips. His best friend, Cameron Jakowski, jabbed him in the ribs with an elbow and gave a low whistle of appreciation. Noah didn't like that one bit. With three sisters and an independent working mother, he'd learned at an early age not to objectify women.

"Who is that?" Cameron asked.

"Fiona."

Cameron raised his brows. "I meant her friend with the great legs."

"Callie Jones," Noah replied quietly.

Cameron chuckled. "The horse lady? Very nice. No wonder you've been keeping her to yourself."

"That's not what I've been doing."

"Sure it is." Cameron smiled. "Shall we go over so you can introduce me?"

"No."

"I just wanna talk to her."

Noah stood perfectly still. "Hard to talk without teeth."

Cameron laughed loudly and began walking toward them. "Okay, I get the message," he said once Noah caught up. "But introduce me anyway."

He did so begrudgingly. Cameron liked women and women usually reciprocated. He was stupidly relieved when Callie seemed oblivious to his friend's brand of charm.

Once the introductions were over Fiona dragged Cameron onto the dance floor. Noah bought a round of drinks and they sat down at a table way back from the noise of the playing band. It wasn't long before M.J. went off in search of the man she'd arrived with and he and Callie were alone.

She looked nervous. And beautiful. He'd never seen her hair loose before. It was longer than he'd imagined and hung way past her bare shoulders. He felt like running his hands through it and tilting her head back so he could kiss her throat.

"You came back," he heard himself say.

She glanced at him. "Yes."

"I'm glad you did."

"It's still not a date."

Her words made him smile, and Noah's whole body thrummed with awareness. Being around her, sharing molecules of space with her, undid him on so many levels. "Of course not. *We* don't date, remember?"

Her blue eyes sparkled. "Do you have to be so agreeable?" she asked quietly.

"Do you have to keep looking for a fight?"

One brow rose sharply. "You like provoking me. It's probably because you were surrounded by women growing up. You know, the spoiled only son, indulged by his mother and adoring sisters, given license to say whatever he wants."

He laughed. "I'm sure my mother would disagree with you."

"Ha—I'd like to talk to your mother," she said and he saw her flush.

"I'm sure she'd enjoy that, too. So where's your family?"

She hesitated for a moment, like she was working out how much to reveal. "California," she replied finally. "My mom lives in Santa Barbara. My brother Scott has a place in L.A," she added. "He works for the fire department."

"And your father?"

"He died ten years ago."

Noah pushed his beer aside. "So why Crystal Point?"

"My dad was born in Bellandale and I vacationed here many times when I was young. After my—" She stopped for a moment. "After I finished professional competition I wanted to do something…else. I'd always wanted to have my own riding school and secured Sandhills Farm for a good price."

"It was a courageous move," he said. "I mean, without family support."

"I had that. I still do."

"Do you miss it?"

"California? Sometimes," she admitted. "But I needed to... to get away."

She'd said too much. He felt it with every fiber inside him. "Get away or run away?"

"Both," she admitted.

"Have you been back?"

She nodded. "I try to get back every year to see my family."

"You're close to them?" he asked.

Callie nodded. "Very."

"But you wouldn't move back to California for good, would you?"

She looked into her glass. "I'm not sure. For the moment this is home."

"That's...good news. For Lily," he clarified. "And the rest of your students." He paused, looking at her. "How many students do you have?"

"Not nearly enough," she replied. "I lost a few a while back. An unhappy client," she explained. "Or an unhappy parent, to be precise."

"Sonja Trent?"

Callie stilled. "You know her?"

"I know her." He took a drink and looked at her over the rim of his glass. "How many more students do you need?"

"To stay afloat?" He could see her doing a quick calculation in her head. "About a dozen or so. I could advertise— but of course that takes money. If I hike up my tuition fees, I risk losing the students I have to one of the bigger equestrian clubs in town who do a group rate. And with insurance costs and the price of feed sometimes I feel like I'm..."

"You feel like what?"

"Like I'm pushing a barrow of manure uphill with a faulty wheel."

He smiled, thinking how he knew that feeling. "I don't think you should dismiss the idea of raising your prices," he said after a moment. "Cheap doesn't necessarily mean value. Sure, your clients could go to the bigger establishment—but would they get what you can give them? Probably not. One-on-one lessons with someone who has your experience is what customers will pay for. Your skills and knowledge make your time valuable, Callie—you've earned the right to be rewarded for it."

Her eyes shone bright with tears, and in that moment Noah wished he knew her better. He saw vulnerability and pain and fought the instinctive urge to reach for her. Now wasn't the time. But soon, he thought. *Soon.*

The compliment went straight to Callie's heart and she fought the sting behind her eyes. Silly, but his words made her feel taller, stronger. Her defenses were down. He broke them down. No, not broke…something else. Somehow he took the barricade around her apart, piece by piece, holding each one of those pieces in his hand, showing her what he had in his palm, drawing her out, making her want and making her feel.

Making me unafraid.

She was momentarily stunned by the intensity of her feelings. What she'd first thought was just attraction suddenly seemed so much more.

She liked him…. She really liked him.

This is a good man, a tiny voice inside of her said. A good man with a dazzling smile and integrity oozing from every pore. A man who made her feel safe when she'd believed no man would ever make her feel that again.

How did she resist? She wasn't sure she could. She wasn't sure she wanted to.

But…to feel again? Where did she find the courage to do that? If she let herself care for him…she would also have to let herself care for his children. She had to allow them inside and into her heart. Into her heart that was only barely glued together these days.

"Callie?"

She realized she'd been staring at him and dropped her gaze. "Yes?"

"Would you like to dance?"

Instinct screamed no. "I can't."

"Yes, you can. It's just a dance."

It wasn't *just* anything…she knew it as surely as she breathed.

"I really—"

"Come on," he urged and took hold of her hand. Before she could protest further he'd pulled her gently from her seat and led her toward the dance floor.

She'd always liked the idea of dancing but had never been all that good at it. Craig had complained it was a precious waste of time when there were horses to train and competitions to prepare for.

The band played covers of popular tunes, and just as they reached the dance floor the beat changed to a much slower number. Callie didn't move at first. At over six feet Noah was considerably taller than her, and she tilted her head back to look at him. Everything about him drew her in. The white collared shirt he wore emphasized his broad-shouldered strength and as she curled her fingers into the soft fabric and felt the hard muscle beneath, every ounce of blood in her veins surged. She hadn't been this close to a man for so long…and never one who'd affected her so powerfully.

The music was slow and they moved well together. One

hand lay gently against her hip and he held her free hand in his. She felt the intimacy right down to her toes.

She took a deep breath. "Noah …" Saying his name set off a surge of feelings inside her. Her body tensed and she knew he felt the sudden shift.

"Yes, Callie."

"Don't expect too much."

He looked at her oddly. "Are we talking about your dancing skills or something else?"

"Something else," she admitted on a sigh and wasn't sure where the words came from. And she wasn't sure she wanted to know. She felt like the worst kind of fraud by denying the obvious and refusing to admit to the feelings running through her.

She was suddenly paralyzed by the realization. It was impossible. She had no room in her heart for anyone. Not him. Not his children. "I have to go," she said a moment later as she dropped her hand from his shoulder.

"I'll drive you home," he said quietly.

Callie stepped back, oblivious to the music, oblivious to everything other than Noah and her furiously beating heart. "I have my truck."

"Then I'll walk you to your truck."

"That's not necessary."

"Yes, it is," he said and continued to hold her hand.

By the time they'd left the dance floor their palms were pressed intimately together. Callie didn't pull away. Deep down, in that place she'd switched off and never imagined she'd switch on again, she found she liked the sensation of his fingers linked with hers. She liked it a lot.

Her truck was parked midway down the car lot and the walk took a few minutes. It was dark and there were a few couples hanging by their vehicles. Callie spotted one pair kissing madly, another simply holding each other. The entire scene screamed of the kind of intimacy she hadn't felt in a long time.

The kind of intimacy she suddenly craved.

She knew it was foolish to want it. She had nothing to offer him other than the fractured pieces of her heart. And for a man like Noah, she knew that would never be enough. He'd want the *whole* Callie. The Callie she'd been before her world had been shattered...before *she'd* been shattered.

And that woman simply didn't exist anymore.

Once they reached her truck she twisted her fingers from his. "Well, good night," she managed to say and shoved a hand into her small bag for her keys.

She found the keys, pulled them out and accidentally dropped them at her feet.

Noah quickly picked the keys up and pressed them into her palm. "Good night, Callie."

She looked at him and saw desire burning in his eyes.

He wants to kiss me...

The power of him drew Callie closer, until they were barely a foot apart. She felt her lips part, felt herself move and felt her skin come alive with anticipation. He leaned in and kissed her cheek so softly all she really felt was breath.

Not enough ...

Callie instinctively reached up, grasped his shoulders and pulled him toward her with all her strength. Driven by instinct, she planted her lips on his mouth and thrust her tongue against his. He tasted good. He felt good.

No...more than that. He tasted...*divine.* And her lips, denied for so long, acted intuitively. She felt her blood heat, felt her skin come alive, felt desire uncurl way down, igniting the female part of her that had lain dormant since forever.

Callie felt his rush of breath as he started to kiss her back. She got the barest touch of his mouth, the barest taste of his tongue. She waited for more. She longed for more. But then he stopped. He pulled away, kissed her cheek again and straightened. Callie released him and stepped back on unsteady feet.

Air crashed into her lungs, making her breathless. She looked at him, felt the burning red-hot gaze. *I know he wants me...*

She knew it, felt it and tasted it in the brevity of his kiss.

"Good night, Callie," he said. "I'll see you Sunday."

Callie got into the truck and started the engine. She wasn't sure how she drove home. All she could feel was the tingle on her lips, the heat in her blood. All she could think was how she had just kissed Noah Preston.

And how her life would never be the same.

Chapter Five

Noah was thinking.

About kisses. About perfect lips and sweet breath.

"What's up with you?" Lily asked, shifting in her seat, looking incredibly young in riding breeches and a dark T-shirt.

Noah looked directly ahead. She'd become way too astute for his liking. "Nothing."

"Yeah...right." She crossed her arms. "I hope you're not gonna hang around while I have my lesson."

"I've got some work to do at the house."

Lily turned her head. "Yeah—that's right. Her place is a real dump." She huffed. "I think you just want to see *her* again. I'm not a little kid, you know. I saw exactly how you were watching her last weekend." Lily rolled her eyes wide. "And she's not bad looking, I suppose, if you go for that type. She's not like my mother."

No one was like Margaret—thank God. But he wouldn't be telling Lily that.

"Do you think you'll ever get married again?"

That was a first. He looked at his daughter. She stared straight ahead, but Noah wasn't fooled. She looked just a little afraid. And Lily never looked afraid.

Married? How could he explain his feelings to his daughter? Noah was pretty sure the younger kids would welcome a new mother into their life. And he…he truly wanted someone to share them with. He longed for a wife and a friend and a lover and all that corny stuff he knew made up a healthy marriage. He wanted what his parents had…years of trust and love. But it was a big deal, expecting a woman to take on four children. And he had no intention of bringing someone temporary into their lives. Noah didn't want temporary. If he got involved again, he wanted permanence. He wanted…forever. He wanted promises that wouldn't be broken. For the kids' sake.

And mine.

His train-wreck marriage lingered like a bad taste he couldn't get out of his mouth.

Is that why I didn't kiss her back…when all I wanted to do was haul her into my arms?

The truth rocked Noah. He'd spent thirty-six hours wondering what kind of fool didn't kiss a beautiful, desirable, passionate woman back when she'd made it so clear she wanted to be kissed. But he knew why. It wound up his spine. It filled his lungs. *Fear.* Fear that he'd want more. Oh, not sex…because he was pretty sure kissing Callie would quickly lead to making love to Callie. He wanted more of *her*. The more of her Noah suspected she wouldn't want to give. To him. To anyone. He didn't want to feel her, taste her and then have the door slammed in his face. He didn't want to be rejected…*left*.

And she'd left before, hadn't she? She'd moved across an ocean to change her life—to get away. From what, he didn't know. What if she wanted to change it back? Noah wasn't going to put his kids or himself through the risk of being wreckage in her wake.

It was best that he hadn't kissed her back. Best that he stopped thinking about kissing her at all.

"So, would you?"

Lily again. Noah got his thoughts back on track. Marriage. Right. "Maybe one day."

She scowled and *harrumphed.* "Do *we* have any say in it?" she asked, using the collective, but Noah sensed she was asking about herself. "I mean, if you're going to shack up with someone, shouldn't we at least be able to have an opinion about it?"

"Marriage is a little more than shacking up, Lily."

She shrugged, looked straight ahead and remained quiet for about twenty seconds. Lily had something on her mind. "Did you know that fifty percent of all second marriages fail?"

He almost choked. *Where the hell did she come up with this stuff?* "That's an interesting statistic, Lily. Where did you get it?"

"Social Studies," she replied. "We're studying human relationships this semester. There's a boy in my grade who's had two stepfathers—can you imagine? And Maddy told me that when her stepdad moved out last year it really sucked. She liked him a lot."

Noah got his daughter's point, delivered with all the subtlety of a sledgehammer. "I have no intention of jumping into anything, Lily," he told her.

"But if you do get married again, how do you know she won't run out like my mother did?"

I don't.

And Callie…she seemed as fragile and unpredictable as the wind.

Lily didn't say anything else, and when they arrived at Sandhills Farm she jumped out of the truck. It took him about ten seconds to find Callie. She stood near the house, in jeans and a flame-red T-shirt, one hand on her hip and the other held a cell phone to her ear.

She spun on her heels and looked at him. His heart pounded behind his ribs. That kiss…how did he forget about it? How could he not want to feel that again? Noah took a long breath and headed toward her. Lily reached her first and jumped around on impatient toes while Callie continued her telephone conversation.

She was frowning and clearly not happy with the caller. When she disconnected a few moments later he pushed aside his lingering thoughts about kissing her and immediately asked what was wrong.

"Just another irresponsible horse owner getting away with neglect," she said hotly.

He frowned. "What?"

"I volunteer with an organization that saves abused and neglected horses," she explained. "A couple of weeks ago I got word that there are three horses somewhere on the other side of town that are stuck in a bare paddock and need veterinary care. We've only had sketchy reports on their whereabouts so far. The owner moves them around to avoid impoundment."

"That's terrible. What can you do?" Lily asked in a shrill voice.

"Seize them, hopefully."

His ever-astute daughter picked up on the obvious. "Isn't that stealing?"

"Not when the owners are breaking animal protection laws."

Lily nodded. "If you need any help, I'll—"

"Leave it to the experts," Noah said. "I'm sure Callie has it under control."

"Your dad's right," Callie assured Lily. "But you can help me nurse them back to health when we finally find them. Joe's saddled Samson for you," she said as she pointed toward the sand arena.

Once Lily headed off, Callie turned to face him. Her eyes were blue and luminous. "I have a list," she said quickly. She pulled a small piece of paper from her pocket and held it toward him. "Of things for you to do." She made a dismissive gesture. "Of course, if you've changed your mind I'll—"

"We had a deal," he said, sensing she was mentally backing out from talking to him as fast as she could. She half shrugged and took a breath, trying to look causal, but Noah wasn't fooled. The tiny pulse at the base of her throat beat like a wild thing. And the promises he'd made to himself only minutes before vanished. All he wanted to do was take her in his arms and kiss her...properly.

"It's only small stuff," she said. "A couple of windows that won't lock right and the back fence—"

"No problem," he said quietly and took the list.

"I'll be about an hour with Lily," she said and pivoted on her heels.

Noah watched her walk into the arena, back rigid, arms held tight to her side. He lingered for a few minutes and observed Callie's interaction with his daughter. Lily looked unusually cheerful and he knew she was excited to finally be in the saddle. The lesson started with Callie laying down a firm set of rules and Lily agreeing to every single one.

Lily respected Callie. Somehow, Callie understood what Lily needed.

Noah experienced a strange pang in his chest, dismissed it and headed for his truck to unload the toolbox. He had a lot of work to do.

* * *

Callie was wound like a spring. She'd barely slept the night before and had struggled to concentrate during a lesson earlier that morning with Maddy Spears, her newest student.

She knew she had to concentrate on Lily…and ignore the fact that Noah was only a couple of hundred meters away.

I kissed him. And he didn't exactly kiss me back.

She wasn't sure whether she should feel relieved or insulted.

"How's this?" Lily asked Callie, interrupting her reverie.

Callie focused her attention on the teenager. She was impressed with Lily. The girl had a natural seat and good hands. Once the lesson had concluded she eased on the long reining lead and called Samson to a halt in front of her.

"That was good. Well done."

Lily raised her brows. "Do I get to ride off the lunge rein next week?"

Callie unclipped the lead. "No."

Lily dismounted and landed on her heels. "Why not?"

"Balance," Callie replied and handed the reins to her.

Lily frowned. "Huh?"

Callie began walking from the arena. "Every rider needs to start with balance. Once I know you've aced it, the lead comes off."

Lily clicked the horse forward and followed. "And what if I don't?"

"You will," Callie said. "You have a good seat and soft hands, essential for a successful rider. Take Samson to the wash-bay and Joe will help you strap him down."

Lily buried her face into the animal's neck and smiled. "I can do it by myself."

Callie raised her brows. "What was rule number five?"

Lily exhaled heavily. "Don't question the four other rules."

"Exactly. Go and get Samson sorted. I'll see you when you're done."

When Lily was out of sight Callie considered her options. Hang around the ménage or show some guts and see what *he* was up to. Her boots made their way across the yard until she reached the house. She stood at the bottom of the steps. Noah had his back to her and she watched him maneuver an old window off its track, make a few adjustments and then replace it. Her heart raced. No man should look that good in jeans. He raised his arms and she got a quick glimpse of smooth skin beneath the hem of his T-shirt. *Oh, sweet heaven.* Suddenly, he stopped what he was doing, turned and looked at her.

"How was it?" he asked.

She gulped. "Huh?"

"Lily—how'd she do?"

Callie put the image of skin out of her mind. "Very good. She's a natural."

He smiled at her and she felt the power of it through her entire body.

"Are you okay?"

It's just skin. I've seen skin before. "Yes," she replied and swallowed. "I'm fine."

He stepped away from the door. "She behaved herself?"

"She did," Callie replied. "She's quite sweet, actually."

He grinned. "Well, I'm pleased the two of you are getting along." He leaned back against the balustrade. "Seeing as that's out the way, are we going to talk about *us* now?"

Callie took a quick breath. *Here we go.* "There's nothing to talk about."

"Yeah, there is."

"It was just a kiss," she said, and the moment she'd said the word *kiss,* she regretted it immediately.

"It wasn't *just* anything, Callie."

He was right. Callie felt it down through to her bones. "Okay," she admitted. "It wasn't."

"So, what shall we do about it?"

Her heart raced. *Do?* "I don't know if we...I don't think we should do anything." She took a deep breath and inhaled a burst of bravado. "We just won't kiss again."

There's that word again... When the word should probably be bliss. Because she suspected that's what really being kissed by Noah would feel like.

He smiled and came down the steps. "I don't think I can make that promise to you, Callie."

Stupidly, she smiled back for a second. "You didn't kiss me back." The words popped out of her mouth. "I figured you weren't interested."

He took another step toward her. "Would you like me to prove to you that I am?"

Callie almost swallowed her tongue. *He is interested...he wants me.* "Right here?" she asked, wondering what kind of madness had taken hold of her.

He shrugged. "Why not?"

Callie took a step backward. He wouldn't, would he? Kiss her out in the open, where anyone could see? Possibly in front of his daughter? She warmed from head to toe. But no...she looked at him and saw he was smiling. "Are you teasing me?"

"Just a bit."

Callie didn't quite know how to react. Teasing and flirting were almost an alien concept to her. Craig had never teased, never flirted. It was always business, always work, always pushing toward being better, being the best. Only now, years later, did Callie realize how little laughter there'd been in their relationship. But Noah had a relaxed sense of humor, a relaxed sense of *self.* She was sure he worked hard—but he didn't live to work. He lived for other things. Like his kids. It would be hard alone, raising four children single-handedly.

Craig hadn't wanted one child.

In the end Craig hadn't lived to see his son born. And Callie had buried them both within days of one another—her tiny son and the man who was supposed to have loved her but instead betrayed her.

The worst week of her life. Excruciating. Soul-destroying. Heartbreaking.

"Where are the rest of your kids today?" she asked, shifting her thoughts from Ryan. And, for some reason, she wanted to know where his children were and who was caring for them.

"With Evie," he replied. "I didn't think you'd want them underfoot while you're working."

"You're right, I don't," she said quickly. Too quickly.

He'd heard the tremor in her voice because his brows slanted together for a brief second. "You don't like kids?"

You don't like my kids...that's what his question sounded like.

Callie shrugged again. *I adore kids,* she wanted to say. *If I had my way I'd have a dozen of my own and love them with every fiber inside me.*

But that was a pipe dream. Ryan was the only child she would ever have. *And I can't replace him. I won't let myself love like that again.*

"I like kids," she said softly.

"Me, too," he said, smiling again. "Can I call you sometime this week?"

Callie was startled. "For what?" she asked, her heart beating wildly.

"Don't look so suspicious," he said quietly. "Nothing sinister."

Callie felt foolish then. "Sorry," she said on a breath.

"I thought you might like to go out sometime."

Like a date? She should run as fast as she could. The idea

of going out with him was terrifying. Because she sensed it was something she could get used to. "I don't…it's just that I'm…I'm better with horses than I am with people."

"And yet you became a teacher?"

She shrugged. He had a point. She could have turned her skills toward training horses for the show circuit. But teaching the kids…that's where she found real happiness.

"Speaking of which, I have to get back to work," she said. "I have a new student starting in fifteen minutes."

His green eyes scanned her face. "Business looking up?"

"Yes," she said quickly. "Much better. I had a new student start this morning, plus three calls yesterday and now four new students starting over the next two weeks."

"That's good news for you."

"I know," she said, a little breathlessly because she always felt as if she didn't have quite enough air in her lungs when talking with him. "When I lost clients following the incident with the Trent girls I wasn't sure I'd be able to recoup. Sonja Trent accused me of discriminating against her daughters and threatened to lodge a complaint with the equestrian federation. Nothing came of it, of course, except she managed to persuade half-a-dozen parents to pull their kids out."

"And then some jerk says he wants to see you lose your license?"

Callie smiled fractionally. "Ah—well, that was a bit of a red flag for me."

"Rightly so, considering the circumstances. I would never have done it, you know?"

"I know," she said, softer this time, feeling like their worlds were moving closer. "I lost my temper. When I called you a jerk I didn't know you." She paused, searching for the words. "I didn't like you. But I know you now. I…like you now."

I more than like you…

"I like you too, Callie."

Her heart beat like a freight train and it was so loud she wondered if he could hear it.

Minutes later he took Lily and left, leaving Callie standing by the porch with a smile on her face so deep her jaw ached.

Lily arrived unexpectedly at Sandhills Farm on Wednesday afternoon, riding her bicycle. She wore her school uniform, sensible leather shoes and her black hair tied back in a ponytail. The uniform looked oddly out of place with her full makeup. "I've come to see Samson," Lily told her when Callie approached her.

"Does your father know you're here?" Callie asked.

She crossed her arms over her chest. "Sure."

Callie began her next lesson with Maddy Spears and Lily began chatting with Maddy's mother, Angela. They seemed to know one another quite well. Her suspicions were confirmed a little later, once Maddy's lesson had finished and Lily came forward with a kind of indulgent authority and steered Maddy and Sunshine toward the washing bay, flipping Callie an assurance that the gelding would be looked after.

Callie gave the girls an opportunity to do the right thing and headed over to speak with Angela Spears.

"You know Lily?" Callie asked, slipping through the fence.

"Everyone knows Lily," she replied. "Another marvelous lesson," the other woman said before Callie could open her mouth. "You are a genius," she said. "Maddy's talked of nothing else but you for days now."

"I'm flattered."

Angela Spears's perfectly bowed mouth beamed at her. Callie couldn't help noticing how immaculately groomed she was. Riding breeches and grass-stained T-shirts had become her usual garb. Too bad—she looked pretty good in a dress.

She hadn't forgotten Noah's reaction the night of the Twilight Fair dance. He'd looked at her dress, and her legs and her mouth…

"Noah was right about you."

Angela's words instantly grabbed Callie's attention. For a crazy second she wondered if she'd inadvertently said his name without realizing it. "What do you mean?"

"He told me you were an amazing instructor."

Her curiosity surged into overdrive. "He did?"

Angela nodded. "And he said I'd be foolish to let Maddy miss the opportunity to learn from you and that she couldn't be in safer hands. Of course, I completely agree now," she said. "And Maddy's so looking forward to getting her own pony." She let out an animated gasp. "Oh, you must help us select the perfect pony when the time comes—I insist. And I'll pay you a finder's fee, of course."

By the time Callie had waved Angela and her daughter goodbye, Lily had disappeared. But she wasn't hard to find. Callie headed for the paddock behind the house and found her sneaking morsels of carrot to Samson.

"So, Maddy's your friend?"

Lily nodded. "My best friend." She gave the gelding another treat.

Callie thought about the three new students she acquired that week. "And what about Jacinta and Skye Burrows and Chrissie Drew—are they friends, too?"

"Nope," Lily replied. "But I think my dad knows Mr. Burrows."

Callie's heart skipped a beat. *He's looking out for me.* It felt like forever since anyone had done that.

Normally she would have resisted the gratitude that coursed through her. On some level she should probably have resented it. Because interference meant involvement. It meant…intimacy. It meant she had cracks in her armor.

But she experienced none of those feelings. Only a deep-rooted appreciation.

And an overwhelming longing to see him again and tell him so.

Callie headed into Bellandale the following morning. She found the address for Preston Marine via the business card Noah had given her and parked outside the large building situated in the center of the town's newest industrial estate. She got out of her truck and ran her hands down her jeans.

She was impressed the moment she walked into the show-room. A long and luxurious-looking cruiser was to her left and three smaller boats, including a catamaran with full sails, sat to her right. Printed designs on easels flanked each of the boats and more designs were framed on the walls. A circular reception area greeted her as she stepped onto the tiled floor and a fifty-something man came toward her. He wore pressed trousers and a shirt with Preston Marine logo sewn onto the breast pocket.

"How can I help you?" he asked politely.

Callie hung on to her nerve. "I'd like to see Noah Preston. Is he here?"

The man, whose name badge read Len, nodded. "He's out back in the workshop."

"Oh," she shrugged. "If he's busy I can—"

"You can wait in his office," Len suggested and walked ahead, motioning her through a door on the left. "I'll call him."

Callie followed with unusual obedience, passing a small, efficient-looking woman who sat behind the reception desk, tapping on computer keys and wearing the same style shirt as Len. When she entered the office Len quickly excused himself, and Callie sat on a long black leather lounge. As far as offices went, this appeared better than most. And it was as neat as a pin.

She didn't have to wait long.

"Callie?"

Noah stood in the doorway, dressed in chinos and the same corporate shirt as his staff. He stared at her with such raw intensity she was relieved she'd been sitting. Her knees would surely have given way if she'd been standing. "Hi."

"Is everything all right?" he asked as he closed the door.

"Oh, yes. I just wanted to speak with you." Callie felt absurdly self-conscious beneath his penetrating stare. "This is a nice office," she said, desperate to fill the silence rapidly smothering the space between them.

"Do you think?" One hand moved in an arc, motioning to the chrome and glass furnishings. "I'm not sure. I've only had this place for about six months. Grace did the decorating. It's a bit too modern for me"

And just who was *that?* "Grace?" she asked as she stood.

"My other sister," he explained.

Stupidly relieved, Callie scanned the room again. "It is modern but appropriate, I think." She relaxed a bit. "You said you'd just moved here?"

He nodded. "I've kept the original workshop down by the Port, but the business needed larger premises."

"And a showroom?"

"Buyers are keen to see the finished product," he replied. "Would you like a tour?"

"Maybe after we've talked."

He closed the door and walked farther into the room. "Okay, let's talk."

Callie clutched her hands together. "I just wanted to...to thank you."

Noah tilted his head. "For what?"

"For Maddy Spears, and Jacinta and Skye Burrows and

Chrissie Drew," she said. "And as of this morning I have another two students starting next month."

He shrugged. "It was only a couple of phone calls."

Callie knew it was way more than that. "It means so much to me," she admitted. "My business…" She paused, and then shook her head. "My horses…"

"They're important to you?"

"They're everything," she breathed.

Noah saw the emotion in her eyes and his chest tightened. "Because they don't let you down?"

She took a shaky breath. "I…I…"

"Someone did," he said and figured there was no point in holding back. "Husband? Boyfriend? Lover?"

"Fiancé," she confessed on a sigh.

"What did he do?" Noah asked, preparing himself for the worst.

She hesitated for a moment. "He lied to me."

Lies and deception went hand in hand—Noah knew that from experience. The fallout from his ex-wife's infidelity had broken his world apart. "Then he wasn't worthy of you."

The emotion in her eyes shined brighter and Noah fought the impulse to reach for her. Everything about Callie affected him on some primal level. He wanted to hold her, soothe her and protect her. He'd never felt such a blinding need before.

She nodded and the gesture spoke volumes. "The horses… they make it simple, you know—uncomplicated." Her hands came together. "Anyway, I just wanted to say thank you for helping me. I guess I'll see you Sunday."

"How about Friday?"

"What?"

"Friday," he said again. "Tomorrow night. Dinner and a movie?"

Callie stilled. "I don't really think a date is—"

He smiled. "Oh, believe me, this wouldn't be a date. Just

you, me, a DVD and the kids squabbling over a bowl of spaghetti."

"Noah, I can't."

"Sure you can," he said easily. "You wanted to thank me—so, thank me." His voice faded for a moment, and then he spoke again. "Dinner, movie, simple."

Silence stretched between them. He expected another refusal and waited for it.

Instead, she nodded and said softly. "Dinner. Yes, okay."

Chapter Six

Noah picked the kids up from Evie's that afternoon. He found his sister and three youngest children in her pottery/art studio, all four of them cutting up cardboard and crepe paper. Pots of glue and an assortment of other hobby equipment lay on the big table in the middle of the room.

They all cheered a round of hellos when he walked into the room and perched on a stool near the kitchenette to the right of the door. Evie left the kids to their crafting and joined him.

"Coffee?" she asked and grabbed a couple of mugs. He nodded and she poured from the pot of filtered brew. "You're early today."

Noah glanced at his watch. "Not by much."

His sister raised her brows. "Bad day at the office?"

"Not particularly." An unusual day. A day filled with thoughts of Callie. Like most of his days lately.

"Trevor has a video-game party planned for tomorrow

night," she said of her fifteen-year-old son. "Do you feel like coming round for dinner? M.J.'s coming over, too."

"I have plans," he said and drank some coffee.

Evie's eyes widened instantly. "A date?"

Noah didn't know what to call it. "Sort of."

"Anyone I know?"

Like a dog with a bone, Noah knew his sister wouldn't let up. Besides, he had nothing to hide about his relationship with Callie. *Relationship?* Is that what it was? It felt…he didn't know what the hell it felt like. Something. Everything. Like she was the air inside his lungs and he couldn't draw in enough breath. His desire for Callie burned a hole through him. *And I haven't even really kissed her.* He'd thought about it, though. He'd imagined it. Dreamed about it. Wanted it so much he could barely think about anything else.

"Callie."

Evie didn't bat a lash. "No surprise there."

"I suppose not." He finished his coffee and stood. "I should get going."

"Sometimes you have to try people on," Evie said quietly. "To see if they fit."

Noah looked at his sister. "That's not the problem."

"So there is a problem?" she asked.

He shrugged and felt like spilling his guts, but he didn't. Because what he felt, what he knew was that beneath the sassy, quick temper and barriers she'd erected around herself was an incredibly fragile woman. A woman who'd been hurt.

I'm going to get my heart kicked in…

That's what he felt deep down. That she was all risk. Like the wildest ride at a theme park. Like parachuting without a chute. But…despite feeling that way, Noah was unbelievably drawn to her. He wanted her, even with the threat of losing himself. And knowing he was prepared to take that chance turned him inside out. Because Noah never risked himself emotionally. He couldn't afford to. The kids needed stability—they needed a parent who could be relied upon to always do the right thing by them. And if he was to bring another woman into their life, that woman had to do the right thing by them also. They needed unreserved love.

Could Callie do that? Could he trust her to love them? He just didn't know.

"There's no problem," he said to his sister. "Thanks for watching them. I'll see you soon."

As Callie zipped up her favorite sundress—the white one with sprigs of tiny blue flowers—and stepped into a pair of silver sandals, she could hear Fiona's voice calling from the kitchen. Her friend had arrived to work her horse and had stayed for a coffee and chat.

"So, you're going on a date with Noah?"

"It's not a date," Callie insisted as she headed from the bedroom. "It's just dinner."

When Callie reached the kitchen Fiona was standing by the sink. "At his home? With his kids?" Her friend raised both brows. "That's a date."

Of course it's a date. I like him. I'm attracted to him.

Just because they weren't going out dining and dancing alone didn't mean it was anything other than a real date.

I shouldn't go. I should keep to my plan and not get involved.

But Callie knew it was too late for that.

She arrived at the Preston home at exactly six o'clock. She grabbed her tote, locked the truck and headed toward the front porch. At the top of the few steps lay a sleepy-looking golden retriever who barely lifted its head at her presence. It made her smile, thinking of Tessa and her boundless energy.

"That's Harry," said a small voice. A young boy stood

behind the screen door. He opened it and stepped in front of her. "He's very lazy."

She smiled "So I see. Not much of a guard dog, then?"

Jamie giggled. "Nope. And he snores really loud." He opened the door and stood to the side. "I'm Jamie—are you coming inside?"

Callie filled her lungs with air and stepped across the threshold.

The polished timber floors, brick-faced walls and warm textures of the furnishings appealed to her immediately. She caught sight of a huge stone fireplace and headed for it, settling her sandaled feet on a thick hearth rug in the middle of the room. The two sofas were covered in a soft caramel color, and a large stone lamp was nudged between them on a round coffee table. The sideboard along one wall was dotted with an assortment of bric-a-brac, most of it obviously created by young, eager hands. The warmth radiating in the room was undeniable and she experienced a deep longing behind her ribs.

"This is the living room," Jamie informed her. "And my TV."

"*Your* TV?" she asked, noticing the huge flat screen and shelving either side showcasing a few hundred movie titles.

"Well, Dad's, really. Do you like spiders?"

"Well, I…"

The sound of feet on floorboards caught her attention, and Callie turned as Noah came down a staircase at the rear of the living room.

He stopped on the bottom step. "Hello."

She hadn't realized the home had more than one level and he must have caught her look.

"The loft," he explained. "The previous owners used it for storage but it seemed a shame not to make use of the view up there, so I had it turned into a master bedroom."

"And bathroom," Jamie supplied.

Noah's bedroom...where he slept. Callie was suddenly rooted to the spot, absorbed by the way he looked in worn jeans and a soft white T-shirt. His feet were bare and it seemed incredibly intimate somehow. His hair was damp, too, and she figured he'd just showered. Which made her think of soap and skin and water cascading over strong muscles. Before Callie could say anything the twins scrambled into the room on fast little feet and planted themselves in front of her.

The little girl touched the hem of her dress. "Callie's here!" she announced excitedly. "You look really pretty. Daddy won't let me wear nail polish."

Callie smiled, amused despite the fierce pounding of her heart. "I wasn't allowed to wear it either until I was..." She paused, looked at Noah and took a gamble. "Sixteen."

Noah smiled. "Good answer." He dropped off the step and took a few paces toward her, his eyes not leaving hers. "You do look lovely."

Eaten up with nerves, she almost told him that he looked lovely, too. But didn't. Because lovely wasn't the word. He looked...hot. And so incredibly sexy in his jeans and bare feet that she had to swallow a few times to regain her composure.

"Okay, guys—give Callie some room to breathe." He moved forward and took Matthew's hand. "I have to get these two in the bathtub. I won't be long. Make yourself at home."

"Where's Lily tonight?"

"At a sleepover at Maddy's," he replied as the trio padded off down the hall.

Callie relaxed fractionally. Until Jamie repeated his question about liking spiders. She had an awful thought he might have one in a jar for her to inspect. Within seconds he was off down the hallway. Callie dropped her tote by the sofa and moved toward the mantel. About a dozen framed photographs caught her attention. Most of them were of the children, and one was of three women. Callie recognized Evie and could see the resemblance in the striking woman beside her with dark hair and perfectly symmetrical features. The other woman, clearly younger, looked familiar, and Callie remembered M.J. from the Twilight Fair. An older couple, his parents for sure because she recognized his mother, filled another shot and then there was a picture of Noah with Cameron, both holding up a fish on a hook and both laughing in a way that only best friends could.

There were no pictures of his ex-wife and she wondered why she thought there might be. Perhaps she just wanted to get a look at the woman who had borne his children and the woman he had loved.

Callie looked at the picture of the twins again and a familiar ache filled her heart.

But she wouldn't think about Ryan tonight...she wouldn't make comparisons. And she wouldn't envy Noah his beautiful, perfect children.

Jamie returned with a heavy book and patted a spot on the sofa. Callie sat down and spent ten minutes listening to him talk about and show pictures of the most hideous-looking arachnids she felt certain would give her nightmares for weeks. But he was a charming boy, polite and very smart and quite mature for his age.

Noah came back into the room without the twins. "They're playing in their bedroom until dinner," he said. He looked at Jamie and smiled. "Hey, mate, how about you go and join Hayley and Matthew?"

"But, Callie has—"

"Seen enough crawlies for one night. Off you go."

Jamie disappeared without another protest and the air thickened between them almost instantly.

"I hope he didn't freak you out too much."

"A little." she said, shuddering. "He's a lovely child. You should be proud of him."

"I am," he replied. "Join me in the kitchen?"

Callie stood and followed him down a short hallway.

The Tasmanian oak kitchen impressed her as much as the rest of the house. She walked to the window and glanced outside. Beyond the patio there was a pool, a hot tub and a gloriously lush garden.

"Would you like a drink?" he asked and grabbed two bottles from a rack above the refrigerator. "Red or white?"

She chose the Merlot and watched as he pulled the cork and poured two glasses.

"Thanks." She took the glass and leaned against the granite countertop. She sipped her wine. "You have a lovely home."

"Thank you. We've only been here a couple of years." He drank some wine, then grabbed a pot and filled it with water. "I bought the place after my divorce."

So his ex had never lived here? She was instantly curious. "Did you have a bitter breakup?"

Surprisingly, he answered. "I guess you could call it that." He flicked on the gas.

Still curious, she asked another question. "Why doesn't she see the children?"

He pulled out a few items and dumped them on the counter. "She lives in Paris with her elderly mother. When she's not in rehab."

Callie gasped.

"Prescription meds," he explained. "Or at least that's how it started for Margaret."

She had a name. "Is that why she left?" Callie asked.

Noah stopped what he was doing and turned toward her. "She left because she didn't want to be married to me anymore." He smiled then but without humor. "Hard to imagine, eh? The addiction started afterward."

Callie allowed herself to hold his gaze.

She felt a strong surge of compassion and deep feeling. But before she could say anything he passed her a paring knife. "Can you make the salad?"

Callie took the knife. "I…I guess. But I should warn you, I'm not much of a cook."

He laughed. "It's salad, Callie—it doesn't need cooking."

"I could still mess it up," she said, trying to push back the color tinting her cheeks.

"Watch and learn."

They worked in silence for a while. Callie chopped and diced vegetables while Noah stirred the sauce simmering in a large saucepan and popped linguini into boiling water.

"That smells good," she said and sipped her wine.

He replaced the lid on the same container. "I can't take the credit, I'm afraid."

She placed a hand to her mouth in mock horror. "Store-bought? I'm devastated."

"Evie," he corrected. "She often doubles up on portions when she has guests staying at the B and B. She takes pity on my single-father status. Actually, I'm pretty sure she thinks I feed the kids macaroni and cheese five nights a week."

"And you don't?"

"Only three nights. Gotta squeeze the frozen pizzas in, too."

Callie chuckled. "Please tell me you're not serious?"

Noah put up one hand in a Boy Scout salute. "I'm not serious. They eat vegetables—even those horrible slimy green ones."

As if on cue, the children returned to the kitchen. Callie remained by the countertop, working on her salad but also watching as Jamie set the table, so serious in his task, his little tongue clicking in his mouth as he straightened cutlery and placed paper napkins beside each place setting. The twins hovered, one each side of her, stepping back and forth on small feet, as though wanting her attention.

She smiled and asked them about their daycare teachers, and Hayley immediately began to tell her everything about a usual day in the classroom. Callie listened, still chopping.

"Can I have some of that?" Hayley asked as Callie cut a carrot.

She nodded and gave them each a little piece of vegetable, which they took with eager fingers and ate just as quickly. A few moments later she did the same with a couple of snow peas. And again with a sliver of cucumber. Their infectious giggles echoed around the kitchen.

"I like having a grown-up girl here, Daddy," Hayley announced and Matthew nodded in agreement.

Callie stopped chopping and stood still. She glanced toward Noah and saw he'd stopped his task also. He was staring at her, a deeply smoldering stare that made her knees weak.

"So do I," he said quietly.

And then, without warning, Hayley hugged her, gripping Callie's leg as hard as her small arms would allow. Callie stilled her task, rooted to the spot. Her heart surged in her chest. Suddenly she was *all* feelings. All anguish. All memory. All hurt. The little girl lingered, waiting, and Callie instinctively knew what the child wanted.

She placed the knife on the counter. *I can't do this. I can't.*

But she did. She reached down and touched Hayley's head, without looking anywhere but directly at the wall in front of her. Her fingertips felt the soft, little-girl hair and her womb contracted instantly, rolling like a wave. Hayley lifted her chin and Callie's hand touched her face.

Oh, God...help me here. Help me not want this. Help me not feel this.

Her throat felt suddenly thick, burning with emotion. All her fears, all her longings bubbled to the surface. She looked at Noah again and sighed. How could she possibly explain what she felt? To explain would mean to be exposed, to be vulnerable, naked in front of him.

Hayley giggled and Callie patted her head gently a couple of times before removing her hand. Once she'd broken the connection her womb flipped again, but differently this time. She felt empty, bereft.

She looked at Noah then and saw he was watching her with such searing intensity she had to lean against the counter for support. But to have his child? An adorable child like Hayley. What a dream that would be.

Not a dream. A fantasy.

"Hayley, take your seat," Noah said quietly. "Dinner will be ready soon."

The kids all whooped and raced for their favorite spot at the table.

"This is done," Callie said and grabbed the bowl.

Meals were usually a quiet affair for Callie. She ate alone most of the time, unless Fiona was around or she offered to make lunch for Joe. But this was something else. The kind of meal she remembered from her childhood, when the kitchen had been the centerpiece of the home. Lots of laughter, lots of spillage and wipe-ups and grubby faces.

Family...

Another woman's family, she reminded herself.

But I'm here...and I feel such a part of them. Like somehow...I was made for this.

Callie's salad was a success, with Jamie kindly telling her it was the best he'd tasted—even better than his Aunt Evie's.

Afterward, she volunteered to load the dishwasher while

Noah put the twins to bed with a story. Jamie chatted to her as she worked, telling her about school and how Fiona was his favorite teacher and how he liked to make things and that he wanted to learn to play the trumpet. Then he told her he would choose a movie to watch and disappeared down the hallway. By the time Noah returned, the kitchen sparkled and the coffeemaker gurgled.

"I helped myself," she said. "Although I can't find any cups."

He opened a high cupboard, extracted a pair of matching mugs and placed them on the counter. "Milk, no sugar."

The way she liked hers, too.

Jamie reappeared, clutching Madagascar in one hand and a Harry Potter sequel in the other. They unanimously chose Madagascar. Callie took her coffee into the living room and sat down in the corner of the long sofa. She placed her coffee on the side table. Jamie said something secretly to his father then excused himself and raced down the hall.

"He likes you," Noah said quietly as he set up the DVD player.

"How do you know that?"

He turned his head and smiled. "You'll see."

Jamie returned a few minutes later. He asked her to hold out her hand and dropped something onto her palm. She stared at the thin leather strip threaded with dark, shiny stones.

"It's a bracelet," he said, pointing to the stones. "They're hematites."

Callie touched the smooth stones. "It's lovely."

"I made it," he announced proudly. "You can have it."

"You made this?" she held it up. "You're very clever. But I couldn't possibly take it."

He looked so disappointed she longed to snatch the words back. "You don't like it?"

Callie rubbed the stones again. "Of course I do. I just thought that if you made something this pretty you might want to give it to someone...like a girl."

Jamie frowned. "You're a girl."

"Smart kid," Noah said as he sat at the other end of the sofa. "My sister Mary-Jayne makes jewelry," he explained. "She lets the kids craft pieces when they stay with her." He looked at his son. "He doesn't part with them easily."

Noah watched her reaction. She looked increasingly uncomfortable. Jamie was a warm, generous child and incredibly easy to love. And although she'd interacted appropriately all evening, he sensed something else was happening to her.

His suspicions were elevated. Was it him making her nervous? Noah couldn't be sure. In the kitchen she'd been relaxed and chatty. When it was just the two of them she usually looked fired up and ready for anything. But then Hayley had hugged her, and Noah had witnessed reluctance in her response to his daughter. The realization landed on his shoulders.

The kids...it was the kids. He felt sure of it.

How can she not like my kids? They're unbelievable. Everyone likes my kids.

Finally, she spoke. "In that case, I would love to keep this. Thank you."

That settled, he flicked the play button and sank back into the sofa. With Jamie between them she seemed light years away from him. Which was probably exactly how she wanted it.

Jamie fell asleep after about twenty minutes. Noah gathered him up and carried him to his bedroom. He tucked him in bed, kissed his forehead and returned to the living room.

She hadn't moved. He flipped the DVD to a CD and

waited until the music filtered around the room before heading back to the sofa.

"Would you like some more wine?" he asked before he sat.

She shook her head. "I should probably go home."

Noah glanced at the clock on the wall. It was barely nine o'clock. He didn't want her to go. He had to say what was on his mind. "I'm not a threat to you, Callie."

She looked into her lap. "I know that."

"So why do you want to leave?"

She expelled an unsteady breath. "Because being here I feel…involved." She stopped, looked away. "I feel involved with you."

Suddenly there was something very raw about her. "Would that be so bad?"

She looked back toward him. "No," she said on a breath. "Yes…I can't—"

"I'm not your ex, Callie," he said bluntly. "And if you screwed up, and if you chose the wrong person to give your heart to, don't feel alone. Just get in line."

"Did *you* screw up?" she asked.

"With Margaret?" he nodded. "For sure. But I should never have married her in the first place." He shrugged. "She was pregnant with Lily," he explained. Not, *I loved her.* To say he'd truly loved Margaret would have been a lie. "We had a baby coming. It seemed the right thing to do."

She smiled fractionally. "It was the right thing to do."

In the beginning he'd believed so. Especially the day he'd held his newborn in his hands. But later he'd wondered if they should have considered a shared custody arrangement of their daughter instead of a marriage between two people who were never suited to one another.

She looked at him, hesitated, and then took a steadying breath. "My fiancé wasn't who I thought he was."

"Was he unfaithful?"

She shrugged. "I don't think so." She dropped her gaze for a moment, then turned back to look at him. "He was killed in a car wreck four years ago."

It wasn't what he'd been expecting and Noah saw the walls close around her as if they were made from stone. A cheating, dishonest spouse was a whole lot easier to compete with than a ghost. "And you're still grieving?"

She gave him an odd look. "Most of the time I'm simply... numb."

He reached across and took her hand. "Can you feel that?" he asked as he stroked her forefinger with his thumb.

She looked to where their hands lay linked. "Yes."

"Then you're not numb, Callie." Noah fought the impulse to drag her into his lap. He wanted her so badly he could barely breathe. "You just fell in love with the wrong man."

She closed her eyes briefly. "I know."

"So maybe we'll both get it right next time."

For a moment she looked like she wanted to be hauled into his arms. He was tempted. Very tempted. But the look lasted only a moment.

She grabbed her tote. He could see her walls closing in, could see her shutting down. "I should go."

He knew the evening was over. "I'll walk you out." Noah stood and followed her wordlessly to the front door. Even with music playing in the background, the house seemed uncommonly quiet. Harry lifted his head when Noah opened the front door, then dropped it disinterestedly.

"Well, thank you for dinner," she said, clutching her bag. "And for part of a movie."

Noah prepared himself for her hasty departure, but she stopped at the bottom step and turned. "I know what you want, Noah. And part of me wants that, too."

The air stuck in his throat. "But?"

"Right now I just…I just don't have room inside myself for any more…feelings."

The raw honesty in her voice was undeniable. He wasn't sure how the brash, argumentative woman he'd first met had morphed into this exposed, vulnerable creature he couldn't take his eyes off. His insides churned. *Don't be afraid of me. Don't be afraid of what's happening between us.* He didn't say it. He couldn't. He wanted to kiss sense into her…to make her really see him, really feel him. But she wanted to run and that annoyed him. *God, this woman's undoing me.*

"Will you ever have room?" he asked quietly.

She looked at him. Through him. "I…don't…I *can't.*"

Moments later he watched her drive away and waited on the porch until the taillights disappeared at the end of the driveway. And he knew he was falling for a woman who'd just admitted she didn't want to feel anything. For anyone. Ever.

Chapter Seven

The familiar sight of Noah's truck arrived at exactly eight fifty-five Sunday morning. Callie was coming out of the stables when she saw him retrieving his toolbox from the tray. She said hello and he said the same, but he quickly headed for the house and began repairing the screen door.

While she was left wondering if he was angry with her, she was also left facing Lily. And Lily was in a dark mood. She grunted when Callie clipped the long lead rein onto the halter secured beneath the bridle. And then again when Callie knotted the reins in the middle of the gelding's neck and instructed Lily to do arm raises.

Lily muttered a "this sucks" under her breath and began her lesson.

It became a long fifty minutes, with Callie acutely conscious of Noah's presence at the house. She wished she knew his moods better. *Was* he angry with her? He worked without breaking; he didn't even appear to look in their direction.

She hadn't heard from him since Friday night. She'd thought he might call. But he hadn't called...and as tempted as she'd been to pick up the telephone herself so she could hear his voice, she hadn't.

"What's up with *you* today?"

Lily's accusing voice vaulted her back to the present. "Nothing," she said.

"You're not paying attention to me," the teenager complained.

Callie switched her mind into instructor mode. "Of course I am. You're doing great." She grabbed a neutral subject. "How did your sleepover go at Maddy's?"

Lily's gaze snapped at her suspiciously as she trotted Samson in a circle, skillfully rising from the saddle in between beats. "How did yours go with my Dad?"

Maybe not such a neutral subject after all!

Callie's face burned. She called Samson to a halt and waited until he slowed before roping him in. Once horse and rider were in front of her she spoke. "It wasn't like that."

Lily's expression remained skeptical. "Yeah, sure."

"I stayed for dinner," she explained. "And then I went home."

Lily didn't like that, either. Her look became as black as her mood. "So you guys are friends now?"

Callie thought about how to answer. "I...suppose."

Lily dismounted. "I thought you were *my* friend?"

Uh-oh. Callie chose her words carefully. "I am, Lily. I have all different kinds of friends."

"Well, *he* doesn't look at you like he wants you to be his friend. He looks at you as if he wants you to be his *girlfriend.*"

Callie grabbed the reins and tried to squash the sudden heavy thump of her heart. *He's not looking at me like anything at the moment.*

"We're *just* friends," she said firmly, unclipping the reigning lead and handing Samson to Lily. "Give him a brush down and ask Joe to get a small feed for him." She caught Lily's scowl. "Horsemanship includes ground work and is all part of learning to ride."

Lily started to move then stopped and swiveled on her boot. "I just don't want things to change, that's all. I like coming here. I like learning how to do stuff."

"Nothing's going to change," Callie assured her, sensing that it was what Lily needed to hear. "I promise."

"So you're like, not moving back to California or anything?"

California? "No."

Lily shrugged. "Because people do move. People…leave."

Like her mother. Callie took about two seconds to figure it out. "Not all people," she said gently. "Not your dad."

Lily didn't look convinced. "Yeah, I guess," she said. "It's not like I don't want him to date or anything…I mean, as long as whoever he dates is not some old witch who hates kids. But you're *my* instructor…and if you went out for a while and then stopped going out, I wouldn't be able to come here anymore. When adults break up that's what always happens."

Callie drew in a deep breath. "We're not dating. We're friends."

Lily nodded but clearly wasn't convinced. Callie remained in the arena until Lily had led the horse into the stables. She wiped her hands down her jeans, tightened the hat on her head and walked toward the house. He wasn't on the porch. The side gate was open and she headed around the back. Noah was by the fence, pulling off a couple of loose palings, while Tessa bounced around his feet.

"Lesson finished?" He spoke before she even made it twenty feet from him.

"Yes. She did a great job. A few more lessons and she'll be ready for her own horse."

He kept pulling at the palings. "I'm nearly done here."

Callie took a long breath and stepped forward. "I was talking with Lily," she said, watching as he kept working. "She knows...I mean, she thinks there's something going on between us," she blurted.

"I'm sure you set her straight."

He *was* angry.

"I said we were just friends."

He glanced at her but didn't respond. Callie took another step and called the pup to heel. But Tessa, the traitor, remained by Noah's side. He popped the palings in place with a few deft swings of the hammer.

"Sure, whatever." He started walking past her but Callie reached out and touched his shoulder to stop him. He looked at her hand and then into her eyes. "What?"

"Exactly," she said, digging her fingers into his solid flesh. "What's wrong?"

He didn't move. "Nothing."

A big fat whopping lie—and they both knew it. "Are you mad or something?"

"No." He still hadn't moved.

"So, we're...okay?"

He shrugged. "Sure."

Callie dropped her hand and felt the loss of touch immediately. He looked tense. More than that...he looked as wound up as a coil.

"Noah," she breathed his name on a sigh. "If you—"

"Just drop it, Callie," he said quietly. "I have to get going. See you later."

She stared after him and watched his tight-shouldered walk with a heavy feeling in her chest. She almost called after him. *Almost.* Tessa followed before she turned back and sat at Callie's boots. She touched the dog's head and the pup whined.

"Yeah...I know what you mean, girl," she said and waited until his truck started up and headed down the driveway.

She lingered for a moment, staring at the dust cloud from the wheels. Once the dust settled she headed back to the stables and prepared for her next student. Fiona called after lunch and made arrangements to drop over later that afternoon. Her final student left at four o'clock and once Joe took off for the day Callie grabbed her best show bridle and began cleaning the leather. Cleaning her gear had always settled her nerves, and she undid the nose band and cheek strap, set them aside and dipped an old cloth into the pot of saddle soap.

It wasn't much of a diversion, though. Because Callie had a lump in her throat so big, so constricting, she could barely swallow. For two years she'd had focus. The farm. The horses. Her students.

And now there was Noah. And Lily. And the rest of his children.

Deep down, in that place she kept for her pain and grief and thoughts of her baby son, Callie realized something that shocked her to the core. *If I reach out, I know in my heart I can make them my own.* She wasn't sure how it had happened so quickly. Feelings hadn't been on her agenda for so long. Now, faced with them, Callie could feel herself retreating.

She wondered if she should have told him about Ryan. Would he understand? He'd had his own disappointments, but he didn't appear to be weighed down with regret and grief. Maybe people *could* move on? Perhaps hearts did mend.

Right then, Callie wanted to believe that more than anything.

But to feel again? Where did she get the strength? Ryan's death had zapped all her resilience. Before that she'd been strong, unafraid, almost invincible.

She was glad when she heard Fiona's car pull up outside and called for her to join her in the tack room. Only it wasn't her friend who stood in the doorway a few moments later. It was Noah.

He was back. And he clearly had something on his mind. Callie got to her feet quickly. Her heart pumped. "Did you... did you forget something?"

He stood in the doorway, his eyes locked with hers. "Do you still love him?"

She was poleaxed. "What?"

Noah was in front of her in three steps. "Your fiancé. Do you still love him?"

"He's dead," she whispered.

"I know. But that wasn't the question." He reached for her, slid one arm around her waist and drew her against him. "The thing is," he said, holding her firm. "If you still love him, I'll do my best to stop...to stop wanting you." His other hand cupped her cheek, gently, carefully. "But if you don't love him, then I'd really like to kiss you right now."

Her insides contracted. "No," she said on a breath.

"No?"

"I don't love him."

His green eyes darkened as he traced his thumb along her jaw. "Good," he said softly.

And then he kissed her.

Callie let herself float into the warmth of his mouth against her own. It was a gentle possession, as if he knew her, as if he'd been kissing her forever. Only one other man had kissed her before this, and as she allowed Noah's lips to part hers, any recollection of that faded and then disappeared. He didn't do anything else—he just kissed her, like he couldn't get enough of her mouth, her taste, her tongue.

Instinctively, Callie's hands moved along his arms and to his shoulders. She touched his hair, felt the silky strands beneath her fingertips and slanted her mouth against his. Finally, when he lifted his head Callie felt so much a part of him she swayed toward his chest. Noah held her still, one hand on her shoulder while the other splayed on her hip and she lifted her chin higher to look into his eyes.

"Noah—I think…" Callie willed herself to move, but found such incredible comfort in his arms she simply *couldn't.*

He didn't let her go, either. "You think too much. How about you stop thinking and just feel?"

Oh, how she wanted to. But her doubts tormented her, taunting around the edges of her mind in a little dance, telling her that taking meant giving. And giving was…giving felt as far out of reach to her as the stars from some distant planet.

He leaned into her, like he knew her fears. "I'd never hurt you, Callie."

In her heart she knew that. "But…but I might hurt you."

"I'll take that risk." He kissed her again, long and slow and deliciously provocative.

Heat radiated through him, scorching her, and Callie wondered if she might melt. Kissing had never felt like this before. Nothing had ever come close to this. He was strong and safe—a haven for her shattered heart.

When the kiss was over she spoke. "But earlier today you were angry with me."

"Yes. No. Not angry…just…wanting you and not sure how to reach you." He touched her face. "Because I do want you Callie…very much."

She wanted him, too. She wanted more of his touch, more of his mouth, his breath. He gave her what her eyes asked for, kissing her passionately, cradling her against his body.

"Hey, Callie! I'm here for—"

Fiona. Noah released her instantly and she stepped back

on unsteady feet. Busted—and by the biggest blabbermouth she knew.

"Oh," Fiona said so chirpily it had to be a cover for her surprise. "Hey, Noah. So…I'll just go and make myself invisible."

Fiona Walsh invisible? Not likely. But to her credit she left the room without another word. Callie looked at Noah. He didn't look the least bit embarrassed that they'd been caught making out. "I should probably go inside," she said quietly. "Fiona is here for…"

"Don't run now."

She twisted her hands together. Her skin, her lips, the blood in her veins felt more alive than she'd believed possible. "Noah…I'm not ready for someone like you."

He stood rigid. "Like me?"

Callie exhaled heavily. "You're like this whole package— like Mr. Perfect." Suddenly the heat was back in the small room, charging the invisible atoms in the air with a heady pulse.

He laughed humorlessly. "I'm far from perfect."

Callie crossed her arms. "I mean that I don't think you're the kind of man a woman kisses and then forgets. I don't think you're the kind of man a woman simply has sex with. I think you're the kind of man a woman makes love with— and I'm not…I can't…"

His eyes glittered. "So this isn't a sex thing?"

Callie blushed wildly. "Well, of course it's a sex thing. I mean, I'm not denying that I'm attracted to you. It's obvious I am. It's not *just* a sex thing."

He didn't move. He stared at her with such burning intensity she had to look away. To the floor. To the side. Anywhere but into his eyes.

Finally, he spoke. "Within minutes of meeting you, Callie, I knew something was happening. I couldn't figure out what, but I knew it was big. I knew, on some level, that it would change my life. But I can't afford to be casual about this. I have a responsibility to my kids to keep myself in a good place and to do the right thing by them."

She took a deep breath as the sting of tears threatened. "That's just it. I know that about you…I feel that. You *have* to think about your children, Noah," she breathed. "And I…I'm not prepared to…I'm not prepared for that."

His gaze narrowed. "For what, Callie? My kids? Is that what you're saying?"

Her heart ached. *I'm saying I'm not ready to let go yet… I'm not ready to forget my baby son and move on. I'm not ready to fall for you and love another woman's children.*

Her heart contracted. "Yes." She whispered the word, knowing it would hurt him, knowing she was pushing him away because she was so afraid of all he offered her. "I don't want a ready-made family."

Silence screeched between them, like fingernails on a chalkboard.

When he spoke, his voice was quiet. "Well, I guess that's it, then. I'll see you next weekend."

Callie stepped forward. "Noah, I really—"

"There's no need to explain, Callie," he said, cutting her off. "I understand what you're saying. You don't want my kids. You don't want me. That's plain enough. I'll see you 'round."

She waited until he'd left the small room before taking a breath. And as she heard his truck pull away, she burst into tears.

Callie remained in the office for a while, but once her tears were wiped up she returned to the house. Fiona was waiting for her on the porch. Her friend sat on the love seat and held two glasses of wine.

"You look like you could use this."

She sank on the seat and took the glass. "Thanks."

Fiona's big eyes looked her over. "You've been crying. What happened? You two looked cozy when I walked in."

"I don't want to talk about it."

"You know," Fiona said, sharper than usual, "sometimes it doesn't hurt to open up a bit. That's what friends do for each other—in case you forgot."

"I'm a terrible friend," Callie said through a tiny hiccup.

"Yeah, I know."

Callie couldn't help the hint of a smile that curled her mouth. "I don't know how to feel," she admitted. "He wants… he wants…"

"Everything?" Fiona asked. "That doesn't seem like such a bad deal to me."

It didn't, no. But taking everything meant giving everything. "I can't."

Fiona took a sip of wine. "You can't live in the past forever, Callie. Believe me, I know that from experience." She leaned back in the love seat. "I know you lost a baby."

Callie gasped. "How do you—"

"I found some pictures," Fiona explained. "Remember when you first moved in and I helped you unpack? You were out with the horses and I was inside going through boxes…" Her voice trailed off.

Her memory box—given to her by the caring nursing staff at the hospital after Ryan had passed away. "Why didn't you say something sooner?"

Fiona shrugged. "I figured if you wanted to tell me, you would. The only reason I'm bringing it up now is that I like Noah. And so do you. I don't get why you'd send him away."

"It's complicated."

"Because he has kids?"

Callie wondered where her friend had gotten all this sudden intuition from. "I'm just not sure if I can do it."

Fiona watched her over the rim of her glass. "You won't know unless you try."

"And if I mess up, the children will be caught in the middle."

"I think you should cut yourself some slack. You're smart and from what I've seen you're pretty good with kids."

"This is different," she said quietly.

"Why? Because you're falling in love with him? With them?" Fiona asked.

Callie gasped. Was it true? Was she falling in love with him? She liked him…really liked him. But love? Could she? Overwhelmed, Callie couldn't find the voice to deny her friend's suspicions.

"Have you told Noah about your son?"

"No."

"Maybe you should," Fiona suggested. "You know he'd understand. Or is that what you're afraid of?"

She stared at her friend. Was that the truth? Was she so afraid of him really knowing her?

"I had a baby," Fiona admitted. "When I was fifteen."

Callie's eyes almost sprang out of their sockets. "What?"

Fiona nodded. "I gave her up for adoption. There's not a day goes by when I don't think about her, when I don't wonder where she is, when I don't pray that the family she's with are looking after her, loving her. I hope they don't love her less because she's adopted."

Thunderstruck, Callie stared at her friend, saw the tears shimmering in Fiona's eyes and pushed back the thick swell of emotion contracting her own throat. She had no idea her bubbly, eternally happy friend was holding on to such a secret. "I'm so sorry, Fee."

Fiona managed a brittle smile. "I guess what I'm saying

is that we all have things in our past that can stop us from looking for happiness or make us blind to it when it comes along. The trick is having the courage to take the chance."

Three days after the afternoon in the tack room, Callie went for a long ride. She rode into Crystal Point and headed for the beach. It was barely ten o'clock and only a few people were about, a couple chasing sticks with their dogs and a lone jogger pounding the sand. She maneuvered Indiana past the restrooms and onto the soft sand. She spotted a couple of small children building a sand castle and urged Indiana to a halt when she heard her name being called.

It was Evie. And the two small children were Hayley and Matthew.

"Hello," Evie said as Callie dismounted.

Hayley came running up to her and hugged her so fiercely Callie was amazed by the little girl's obvious display of affection. Evie stood back and watched the interaction keenly as Hayley showed off her thumbnail painted with transparent glitter polish compliments of her Aunt Mary-Jayne.

Both kids hovered around Indiana, and he stood like an angel while the little girl patted his soft muzzle. Matthew was a little more reluctant, but after a small amount of coaxing from his aunt he stroked Indy's shoulder.

"He's such a beautiful animal," Evie said with a whistle.

Callie smiled proudly. "Yes, he is." The kids lost interest in the horse and headed back to their sand castle. "They look like they're having fun."

Evie smiled. "They love the beach. I try to bring them as much as I can."

"Do you look after them often?"

"Every Wednesday," she replied. "My mother has them on Fridays and the rest of the week they're in daycare." Evie looked at the twins affectionately. "They're off to school next year and I'm already missing them just thinking about it."

Callie stopped herself from watching the twins. "They're lucky to have you in their life."

Evie shrugged. "They're easy to love."

Yes, Callie knew that. And she could feel herself getting drawn toward them. Evie patted Indiana for a moment and then slanted Callie a look she knew instantly would be followed by a question. "So, are you and Noah seeing each other?"

"Where did that come from?"

Evie smiled. "Jamie said you make a mean salad."

Callie tipped her Akubra down on her forehead.

"I knew you were going on a date. But I was surprised when the kids told me you'd been to the house," Evie said when she didn't reply. "You're the only woman he's invited home to be with his kids since his divorce. I figured that meant something."

Callie remembered Hayley's innocent remark about *grown-up girls* and her insides contracted. She'd known it, felt it...but to hear the words, to know he'd never had another woman in the house with his children...it made her heart ache.

"He's a good guy," Evie said quietly. "He had a tough time with his ex and deserves to be treated right."

Callie managed a brittle smile. "Are you warning me off?"

Evie chuckled. "Lord, no. And Noah would strangle me if he knew I was talking with you about this. Sometimes I get into my protective-sister mode and put my foot in it. But I like you, Callie. And I love my brother. So you can tell me to back off and stop meddling if you want—but I probably won't listen."

Callie was surprised by the other woman's frankness. "I hear you."

"She didn't want her kids, you know," Evie said as she looked over toward the twins. "Imagine that. I mean, she had a lot of emotional problems, no doubt about it…but to just walk away from two new babies…it's unfathomable to me." She sighed. "And Jamie was barely more than a toddler himself. As for Lily…sometimes she acts so impulsively and I'm concerned she has abandonment issues. And you'd never really know what Noah is thinking. But I guess when your wife packs her bags and tells you she doesn't want you or your children—it must make it hard to trust someone again."

Callie's breath caught in her throat and emotion burned behind her eyes.

Abandoned, motherless children…and a good man trying to hold it all together. She suddenly felt the shame of what she'd said to him right down to the soles of her boots.

She'd said the words to hurt…said them knowing they would hit him hard.

She'd wounded him instead of doing what she should have done…which was to tell him the truth. About why she was so afraid. Fiona was right—she needed to tell him about Ryan.

"I have to go," she said as she grabbed the reins and sprung into the saddle. "Thanks, Evie," she said as she turned Indiana back toward the boat ramp and began the quick canter home.

Twenty minutes later she was back at Sandhills Farm. She untacked Indiana, turned him into one of the small paddocks behind the house and then headed inside. One telephone call and a change of clothes later and she was on the road.

She'd called Preston Marine and was told Noah was working from home that day. Within eight minutes she'd pulled her truck into his driveway. Callie turned off the ignition and got out. She heard a loud noise, like a motor running, and followed the sound around the side of the house. She saw him immediately, behind the pool fence holding a chainsaw.

In jeans and a white tank shirt, he looked hot, sweaty and gorgeous. She observed for a moment as he cut branches from an overgrown fig tree and tossed them onto a growing pile. There was something incredibly attractive about watching a man work—a kind of primitive instinct, purely female and wholly erotic. As if aware he was being watched, he stopped the task, lay the chainsaw aside and turned. He walked around the pool and came to a halt about ten feet from her.

"Hello."

She took a breath. "Hi."

He looked at his hands. "I need to wash up."

Callie followed him through one pool gate and then another until they reached the patio. She waited while he slipped through the back door and then returned a few minutes later, cleaned up and in a fresh T-shirt and carrying two cans of soda.

He pulled the ring tab and passed her one. She took it, desperate to touch his fingertips, but she didn't. "Are you playing truant today?"

"Just working off steam."

Callie suspected she was the steam he needed to work off.

He put the can down on a nearby table. "Why are you here, Callie?"

She held her breath. "I saw your sister today."

His brows came up. "Did she embarrass me?"

"No." Callie stepped back on her heels. "But she said something. She said…she said you'd never invited a woman here…to be with the kids. Before me."

"She's right."

Another breath, longer, to steady nerves stretched like elastic. "Why not?"

He pulled out a chair for her to sit on and then one for himself. Once Callie was seated he did the same. Finally, he spoke. "When you're treated badly, when the person you've committed yourself to walks out the door and says she doesn't want you, she doesn't want your children, she just wants to be free, it breaks something inside you. It broke something inside *me*," he admitted. "I have no illusions about the kind of marriage I had. Most of the time it was a disaster. She'd left once before—the second time I told her that was it, no more. She had to make a choice. And she chose freedom." He leaned forward and rested his elbows on his knees.

Callie stood and walked across the patio. She looked at the pool and the immaculate garden and the timber cubby house she knew he would have built himself. When she'd gathered the courage to say what she come to say, she turned. He was still seated.

"I'm so sorry, Noah." Callie inhaled heavily. "About what I said the other day. I know I…I hurt you."

He didn't move.

Callie took a deep breath. "The way it came out, the way it sounded… That's not what I wanted to say. And certainly not what I meant."

He stood up and walked toward her. "So what did you want to say?"

She placed her hand on his arm and immediately felt the heat of their touch. "That your kids are amazing." She swallowed hard and kept her hand on him. "What I'm feeling, it's not about them. It's about me."

Noah covered her hand with his. "What *are* you feeling, Callie?"

Callie looked at him and her eyes glistened with moisture. She inhaled deeply, taking as much into her lungs as she could. "The reason I feel as I do…the reason I push people away…" She paused, felt the sting of tears. "The reason I push *you* away…it's because I lost someone."

Noah's grip on her hand tightened. "Your fiancé?"

She met his gaze levelly. And the tears she'd been fighting tipped down over her lashes. "No, not Craig."

"Then who? What do you—"

"My son," she whispered. "My baby."

Chapter Eight

"You had a son?" The shock in his voice was obvious.

Callie shuddered. "His name was Ryan," she said and felt the hurt right through to her bones. "He died when he was two days old."

She watched Noah think, absorb. "How long ago?"

"Three years," she said quietly and inhaled. "Ten months... one week...three days."

He swallowed hard. "How? Was he sick?"

She shrugged and turned, wrapping her arms around herself. "I was in an accident." She hesitated, took a long breath and then looked at him. "A car wreck."

Noah clearly knew what that meant. "The same one that killed your fiancé?"

"Yes."

She watched as the pieces of the puzzle came together in his head. "You lost them both?" He turned her back around and rubbed his thumb along her jawline. "Why didn't you tell me this before now?"

She looked down, taking a breath. "Because I don't talk about it. And we haven't known one another very long and I didn't…couldn't… Well, being responsible for someone's death, it isn't exactly the kind of thing I want to talk about."

Noah didn't try to hide his shock. "How were you responsible?"

"The accident," she replied. "It was my fault."

"Were you driving the car?"

She shook her head. "No, Craig was driving."

"Then how could—"

"I distracted him," she admitted. "I made him lose concentration. And I shouldn't have. I was angry because we argued." She didn't say anything for a moment. She looked up and around and then back to him. "Craig didn't want the baby."

"He didn't?"

"No. He didn't want anything other than to use me. I fell for him when I was seventeen," she explained quietly. "I moved in with him, wanted to be with him. Craig trained me, taught me everything I know. He was a gifted rider. I thought he loved me. But I found out too late that he only cared about his career. *Our career,* as he called it." Another breath. "We'd worked hard, trained hard, put in hours and used all our money. The Grand Prix Championships were at our fingertips—and after that, the big one, the Olympics, every rider's dream. But I got pregnant and everything changed. I couldn't ride, I wouldn't risk riding. Craig was furious. I'd never seen him like that. We argued about it for three days. In the end, he told me I had to make a choice."

She paused, took a long breath, gathered herself and blinked away the fresh tears in her eyes. "He wanted me to end it. The pregnancy."

Noah's mouth thinned. "What did you do?"

"Moved back in with my mom."

"And then?"

"I decided to get on with my life. When I was about five months along, Craig came back. He said he wanted to try and work things out. He said he'd changed his mind about the baby, about me. And I believed him."

She knew he heard the "but" in her voice. "What happened then?" he asked.

Callie shrugged. "For a few weeks it seemed like it would be okay. And as much as I felt betrayed by Craig, I knew my baby deserved a father. Craig even talked about setting a date for the wedding." She paused, thinking, remembering. "On the day of the accident he came around early. We talked about me moving back in with him, about turning one of the guest rooms into a nursery. He asked me to go for a drive. I was happy to do it, happy thinking everything would work out. We got in the car and drove for a while. But he seemed edgy to me, like he had something on his mind. And then... and then he said it. He said it and I knew I could never trust him again."

Noah held her tighter. "What did he say?"

"My horse," she replied. "He wanted my horse, Indiana. That was what he wanted. That was *all* he wanted. Not me, not our baby. You see, Craig was a gifted rider with a good horse, where as I was a good rider with a gifted horse. He wanted to ride Indy in the Grand Prix qualifiers. He said if I loved him, if I wanted him to be a part of my life, and the baby's life I had to do what he asked."

"And the crash?" Noah asked quietly.

"He was furious with me, called me a few names. He tried to touch me and I pushed him off." Her voice cracked, sounding hollow. "He lost control of the car. We ended up crashing into a guardrail and down an embankment."

Noah winced. He felt pain and rage rip through him. Anger toward a man he'd never met. A dead man. A man who'd hurt this woman so much, who'd broken her to a point Noah feared she'd never be whole again.

"Was he killed instantly?" he managed to ask, though he didn't know how. His heart thundered in his chest.

She nodded. "Yes."

"And you?"

"I was rushed to the hospital," she said. "I had a lot of internal injuries and the baby was in distress. I was pretty out of it. My mom was there and they told her there were no guarantees for either of us. So the doctors delivered him." Tears came again, brimming over. "He fought for two days. He was so tiny. I was so sick and only got to spend a moment holding him."

Noah swallowed, fighting the emotion in his throat. It was every parent's worst nightmare. And she'd endured it alone. He wished he could turn back the clock and be there with her, hold her through every awful moment. He took a deep breath. "I can't even imagine how you must feel."

Callie looked at him. "Ashamed that I didn't see through Craig's lack of integrity. If I had, maybe Ryan would still be alive, maybe my beautiful boy would be with me. He'd be nearly four years old now."

Four years old...

Noah drew a sharp breath. And the truth hit him with the force of a sledgehammer.

"The twins..." His words trailed and then picked up. "That's why you... Ah, of course."

Her throat convulsed. "Sometimes...it's hard to be around them."

Because they reminded her of all she lost.

"I'm so..." He stopped, searching for the words. Everything he considered seemed grossly inadequate. "Thank you for telling me," he said, and even that wasn't nearly enough.

"I needed to," she said, and Noah felt her pull against his

embrace. He let her go and she walked back to the seat and dropped into it. "I wanted you to understand that what I'm feeling is about *me*. Not them. Not you."

That didn't sound right. Her resistance, her pain was about him. And the kids. She'd lost her baby—and that loss stopped her from wanting to *feel* again. Noah could see her struggle. He could feel it. But he wasn't about to let her walk away from him.

He returned to his seat and grasped her hand. "Callie," he said gently. "What do you want to happen between us?"

She looked uncertain and he felt panic rise in his blood. He wanted her to say she wanted everything—him, the kids, the life he knew was within their reach. But her silence was suddenly deafening.

Finally, she spoke. "I've done a good job of putting my emotions on hold for the past few years. And as much as I'm drawn to you, Noah, I just don't know if I'm ready to feel again."

His fingers tenderly rubbed her knuckles as he kissed her. "I'm no expert, Callie," he said against her mouth. "But if you feel anything like I'm feeling right now, we're off to a good start."

She moaned slightly and the sound undid him. He wanted her so much. Needed her so much. He felt like saying something to her, maybe tell her exactly what she meant to him. Something uncurled in his chest, thudding loudly. *Liking* Callie, *desiring* Callie had swiftly turned into something else. And this Callie—this beautiful, fragile woman who now trembled in his arms, was suddenly the one woman he wanted for the rest of this life.

"Callie?"

She looked up. And one look did it. One look from blue eyes shimmering with tears.

I'm gone...

The feeling reached right through to every pore in his skin, every blood cell, every scrap of air that filled his lungs when he took a breath.

"Spend Saturday with me," he said quietly. He kissed her again, slanting his mouth over hers in a sweet, possessive caress and he felt her tremble. "Can you rearrange your lesson schedule?"

"Yes." She sighed. "And thank you for understanding."

He nodded. He did understand. She wasn't a woman to be rushed. And because he'd waited his entire life to feel this way, he'd do his best to give her whatever time she needed.

Wear a swimsuit.

Callie hadn't asked him why he'd insisted she make sure she had a bikini underneath her clothes for their date Saturday. However, when she spotted two long objects secured to the racks on the roof of his truck she knew why.

She frowned. "Boats?"

"Kayaks," he corrected and opened the passenger door.

"I don't really do boats."

He laughed deliciously. "It'll be fun," he said. "Trust me."

"I do," she replied. "I just don't trust boats."

He told her M.J. had arrived early that morning and was happily in charge of the kids for the day. Jamie had insisted on making Callie a matching pendant to go with the bracelet he'd gifted her and Callie was incredibly touched.

The trip to the boat ramp took about ten minutes and Callie relaxed. The nervous energy she seemed to have around him had disappeared. She felt calm and happy. And Callie sensed she was ready for the next step. Telling him about Ryan had been exactly what she needed to do. It gave her strength and, from somewhere, the courage to dare to imagine a future with the incredible man beside her.

When they reached the boat ramp he passed her something. "You'll need to wear this. There's a ladies bathroom over there."

He pointed to a concrete block building about fifty meters away. *This* turned out to be a black, stretchy, sleeveless wet suit that came to her knees and a pair of matching shoes with rubber grips on the soles. Once out of her jeans and shirt and into the wet suit, Callie ran her hands over her hips. With only a bikini beneath, she felt a little deliciously decadent. When she returned to the truck she saw he'd also changed into a similar suit.

It should be illegal for a man to look that good in black rubber.

She watched, feeling rather useless, as Noah unclipped the kayaks from the utility, prepped them for their outing and launched them into the water.

"Ready?" he asked and handed her a sun visor. It looked new, as if he'd bought it especially for her. "Can you swim?"

"Yes."

"Good," he said and passed her a life jacket. "Humor me anyway and wear this."

Callie didn't argue and slipped the jacket over her wet suit.

"We'll go up river," he said. "It's low tide at the moment. Just stick close by me."

She didn't intend to let him out of her sight.

Noah gave her quick but detailed instructions on how to use the single oar and maneuver the craft through the water. Half an hour later they were on their way.

Noah stayed at her pace and they paddled up river, splicing through the water in unison. On either side of the river the mangrove branches twisted and rose up onto the sandbank. Schools of fish crisscrossed below them and some flipped out of the water, delivering a salty spray across her face and arms.

"How are your arms holding up?" Noah asked after about an hour.

"Good. Although I think I'll be sore tomorrow."

"We'll stop for a bit," he said. "I owe you breakfast for making you get up this early."

Callie laughed. "Breakfast? Is there a café tucked along here somewhere?"

"You're sitting on it," he said, grinning. "There's a storage compartment beneath your seat. There's a cooler with food and a thermos of coffee."

Callie looked between her legs and chuckled. "So, what are you sitting on?"

He laughed. It was a rich, lovely sound. "The first-aid kit. Sunscreen. A spare life jacket. And my phone."

"You've thought of everything."

"Habit," he said, and indicated her to turn the kayak toward a smaller secluded inlet. "With kids you have to be prepared for any emergency."

Noah pointed to a tiny alcove ahead and they oared to shore. He got out first and dragged his kayak onto the sand and quickly helped Callie do the same. Once her feet hit the ground she felt the wobble in her calves and thighs. Noah grabbed her by the shoulders.

"Sea legs," he said with a smile. "It'll pass."

Callie let the warmth radiate through her. His fingers were strong and gentle against her skin. She placed her hands at his waist. That felt good, too. She wished she'd tossed off the life jacket so she could get closer to him. Then he kissed her with all the pent-up passion fuelling the long three days since they'd seen one another.

"Callie," he whispered against her mouth, before he kissed her cheek and the delicate and sensitive skin below her earlobe. "I'm starved."

She smiled. "Me, too," she admitted, not wanting to leave

his embrace but liking the idea of some food. She pushed past the nagging disappointment she felt when he released her. "What did you bring?" she asked as she slipped off the life jacket.

"Let's see."

They unpacked the kayak together. Callie grabbed the small rug he'd provided and spread it down farther up the bank in a spot shaded by a wiry native tree. She sat with her knees up, while Noah stretched out his long limbs beside her. There was fruit, soft bread rolls, cheese and smoked ham. They sat on the rug, eating and not saying much of anything for a while. Noah passed her a resin mug filled with coffee and she took it gratefully.

The weather was warm with a gentle hint of breeze and there were birds calling out from the trees above. Water lapped at the edge of the small sandy inlet and the sound was faintly hypnotic.

She put down her mug and uncurled her legs. "It's a lovely spot. Do you come here often?"

"Not much."

He wasn't looking at her, she noticed. He was looking at the sand, his feet and the drink in his hand. She said his name again and he looked up. His green eyes were vibrant and wholly aroused. Heat rode up her spine at a galloping speed.

"I didn't," he said quietly, interpreting her response, "bring you here with any motive other than to spend time with you."

"I know." Callie rested back on her elbows, felt the wet suit stretch with her movements and saw his gaze narrow. "I also know you won't rush me."

He sucked in a breath. "I'm glad you know that."

She relaxed fractionally. Dare she admit he was first man outside of her family who made her feel safe? "It's not that I'm afraid of…of…" She waved her hand between them.

"Of making love?"

"With you?" She pushed herself up and let out a long breath. "No. It's just that I've only ever been with one man in my whole life and it seems like such a long time ago."

"There's no hurry."

Noah looked so calm and controlled. But Callie wasn't fooled. He wanted her. Yet she knew he wouldn't take what she wasn't ready to give willingly. "There isn't?" she queried with a husky breath. "You're right."

His eyes glittered brilliantly. "You know, you're looking at me like that isn't helping my good intentions."

"Sorry," she said on a breath. "I guess I'm out of practice at all this."

"Don't be sorry."

The steady sincerity of his gaze raced directly to her heart. "Noah, I wish I was—"

"Come here," he directed softly. "Stop thinking. Stop talking. Just come here."

Callie resisted for a nanosecond and then she was in his arms. Noah captured her mouth in a deep, soul-wrenching kiss. She gripped his shoulders as he rolled her half on top of him. Their legs tangled and he grasped her hips, bringing her closer to the length of his body. "You're so beautiful," he whispered against her mouth.

Callie flung her head back and allowed him to trail hot kisses across her collarbone. She could feel him hard against her and her thighs parted, arching into his body. He touched her arms, her shoulders, her hands. He touched her over the wet suit, cradling her hips. Callie's hands curled over his biceps and she sighed against his mouth. Touching him became as intrinsic as breathing. They kissed and kissed, absorbing one another. Noah rolled over in one swift move, lodging a leg between hers. Callie could feel the force of his erection and it fueled her desire, driving her to kiss him more, touch him more. She sighed, a deep shuddering sound that echoed through them both. She heard him groan, felt the rising urgency in his touch, knew that he was as driven by need as she was. He kissed her as he tugged the wet suit off her shoulders. He cupped her breast through the thin fabric of her bikini top and Callie felt a flood of moisture between her thighs, a longing deep down, driving her to want more, need more. Her hips rose in anticipation, waiting, wanting and screaming with need. She reached down to touch him, felt him hard against her palm, felt the power in her hands as he grew harder still against her stroking fingers. It was as if they had been doing this forever—as if they had known one another in another time, another life.

"Callie," he muttered, like the word was ripped from his throat. "We have to stop."

She put her hands into his hair. "No, please."

"We have to stop," he said again, raggedly. "I don't have a condom. I can't protect you."

She clung to him. Some faraway voice told her he was right. But she wanted him so much. "It's okay," she breathed.

"No," he said, more groan than anything else. "It's not. I won't...I won't make you pregnant. At least, not like this. Not here. And not yet."

Callie's heart stilled, and pain filled every part of her chest. She felt herself move, retreat, pull away. She had to tell him of her pain. Her shame. "You're right, Noah," she whispered, suddenly cold. "You won't make me pregnant." A shuddering sigh came out. "I can't have children."

Noah pulled back immediately. He felt her hurt through to the blood in his bones.

She can't have children.

The pieces of the puzzle of who she was fell spectacularly into place. Of course. It made so much sense. Her son had died and she'd never have another.

Then share mine burned on the edge of his tongue. He wanted to tell her, make her see that she could have children if she wanted them. His kids, who would welcome her into their life. He knew it as surely as he breathed. Even Lily. They *needed* her. *He* needed her.

She scrambled up and took a few moments to readjust her clothing. Once she'd pushed her wetsuit back up she began collecting the leftover foodstuffs and blanket.

Noah adjusted his own wet suit and moved behind her. "Callie?"

She shook her head as she picked up the blanket and began folding. "I'd really rather not talk about it."

"I think we should," he replied, not touching her but so close he felt her nearness like a magnetic field.

"I can't have kids," she said, folding and refolding. "That's really all there is to it."

"Because of the accident?"

She turned around and faced him. "Yes." A simple response to a complicated situation. And not nearly enough. He looked at her and she continued. "I had a lot of internal injuries. The doctors told me I have about a ten-percent chance of ever carrying a baby to full term."

He stared at her. "So you can *get* pregnant?"

Obviously not the question she was expecting. "Well—yes, I suppose. I just can't stay pregnant."

"Then we did the right thing by stopping."

"I guess we did," she said stiffly.

Noah took the blanket from her. "We did, Callie. Come on," he said quietly. "The tide is coming in, we should get going."

They barely spoke on the trip back. When he dropped her home he stayed for a coffee he didn't really want. On the porch, with Tessa at his feet, Noah felt the tension of unfulfilled desire beat between them like a drum.

"You were right," she said unsteadily before she sipped her coffee. "We were sensible to stop. I don't think I could bear to get pregnant only to lose...to...well, you know what I mean. I guess that's why I tell myself I can't have children. It's easier to cope with."

"Ten percent is still ten percent," he said soothingly. "It's a chance."

She shook her head. "No. It's too big a risk. I didn't really think a lot about children before I found out I was expecting Ryan. I guess I just took it for granted." His gaze narrowed and she explained. "The feeling that a little piece of you keeps going on because of your children... It wasn't until I was told I wouldn't be a mother again that I realized just how much I really wanted it." She sighed heavily. "One of life's base instincts, I suppose."

Noah set down his mug and grasped her hand. "There are many ways to become a parent, Callie," he said and suddenly felt like spilling his guts and telling her everything about his disastrous marriage and Margaret's infidelity.

She shrugged. "I suppose."

It wasn't the response he hoped for. "You don't believe that?"

"I think...I think someone with four children wouldn't really know what I feel."

He stood up and walked to the stairs, turning around to face her with his hands on his hips. "And you once accused *me* of being arrogant," he said pointedly.

"What does that mean?"

"It means that you didn't corner the market on lousy relationships."

"I didn't say I had."

"But you imply it," he said quietly, completely frustrated. "I'm not going to pretend to fully grasp what it must have been like for you to lose your baby...or how it feels knowing you might never have another child. But despite what you might think, I do know a bit about disappointment…and loss."

Her blue eyes shone. "Because of your wife?"

"Because I married a woman I didn't love and who didn't love me," he replied. "And she spent the next ten years punishing us both for it. But I stuck with it because I'd made a commitment and I felt I owed my children a chance at a normal life with parents who stayed together." Noah dropped his arms to his sides. "It was a train wreck from the very beginning."

"But you stayed?"

"I stayed for the kids," he said honestly. "They needed me."

She stood up and reached him in a couple of steps. "You were right to stay," she said. "For Lily's sake especially. She's afraid, you know. Afraid you might leave."

Noah's chest hurt. "She said that to you?"

"She implied it. I think Lily is frightened things are changing."

"Change is inevitable, though."

Callie nodded. "I suppose. I'm not an expert on teenage girls, Noah, but I was one once. And in a way I understand what Lily is feeling. My father was sick for a long time before he died. And even though I knew my mom wasn't sick and wouldn't die, too, part of me always feared that she might. So maybe you simply need to talk to Lily and tell her you're not going anywhere."

Strange how good it felt to talk to her about Lily. The years of going it alone had been lonely ones. He could easily imagine Callie at his side, every day, every night. "Thank you for caring about Lily."

"I do care," she said quietly and looked away.

Noah stepped closer and took hold of her chin, lifting her face up. "But you're not sure you want to, right?"

"Honestly...being around you makes me more confused than I've ever been in my life." Her hands found his chest. "Would you...would you like to stay for a while?"

"Yeah," he breathed. "But I have to pick the kids up before three."

"Oh." Disappointment etched on her face.

"Evie's got guests arriving at two," he explained. "And my folks are golfing all day."

She moved her fingertips. "Another time, then?"

He grasped her shoulders and looked at her. "I *want* to stay with you." He pulled her close and her hands were imprisoned between them. "Believe me." One hand moved over her shoulder and he gently touched the back of her neck and tilted her head fractionally. "I want to make love to you so much I can barely think about anything else." Especially after what had happened between them down by the river. "I'll call you later," he said, kissing her. "And of course I'll see you tomorrow, for Lily's lesson."

"Of course," she whispered.

He kissed her again and the feel and taste of her was imprinted all over his skin. And Noah knew, without a doubt, that he wanted to love her for the rest of his life.

Only, he had no idea if Callie wanted the same thing.

Chapter Nine

Callie hitched the trailer to her truck and got Fiona to check the lights. Her friend gave her the thumbs-up.

"Can I *please* come with you?" Lily asked for the third time.

"Like I said the first time, no."

Lily scowled. "But I could help. You might need me."

Rescuing the three neglected horses would be tricky, but it needed to be done. Because Animal Welfare hadn't been able to trace the horses, Callie and Fiona had found out their location through a mutual friend and horse trainer. They'd planned the rescue for late Wednesday afternoon and would inform the authorities when they had the animals loaded on the trailer. Only Callie hadn't expected Lily to turn up and insist on helping.

"Definitely not," she said. "Get your bike and head home."

"Dad will let me go if I ask him," Lily said.

Callie looked at her. "No, he won't."

She knew how Noah would react. He was a stickler for doing the right thing. And what they were doing was not exactly protocol—even if their intentions were noble. She'd considered telling him about her plans because she didn't want there to be any secrets between them. But Fiona talked her out of it, insisting the fewer people who knew the better.

"But I *want* to help," Lily insisted and then said with a pout, "I thought we were friends."

"We are," Callie said, firmer this time. "But your father is—"

"More than a friend," Lily said bluntly and pouted again. "Yeah, I get that. I'm not a little kid. I know you guys are into each other."

Callie tried to ignore the heat climbing up her neck. She suspected Lily knew about their kayaking trip. Well, not everything. But Lily was smart, she'd work it out, even if Callie was reluctant to come clean and admit she and Noah were together. "I was about to say that your father wouldn't want you mixed up in this. And neither do I," she added.

"I can take care of myself," Lily said and crossed her thin arms. "And I wish everyone would stop treating me like I'm five years old. I'm thirteen...old enough to...well, old enough to do lots of stuff. And it's not like I'm about to go and do something stupid. And the way my dad's been acting lately, you'd think I was some sort of glass doll."

Callie caught Lily's resentment. "He's concerned about you."

"No need," the teenager replied. "I get that he wants a girlfriend," she said and flashed her eyes at Callie. "But who says it would work out anyway? I mean, people get together and break up all the time, right? Even married people. *Especially* married people. In fact, I don't know why adults bother to get married at all. They should just have kids and break up straight away...that way the kids don't have to get used to the idea that having parents who are together is normal."

Once she'd finished her impassioned speech, Lily bit down on her lower lip. Callie's concerns about Lily's fragile emotions increased tenfold. For all the girl's bravado, she wasn't fooled. Lily was hurting. Lily felt things deeply. And Callie knew the young girl was concerned about her relationship with her father. Noah was all she had, Lily's rock, the one constant in her life. And Callie had no intention of threatening that foundation.

"Time for you to go home," Callie said gently. "I'll see you on Sunday."

Lily begrudgingly accepted her decision and took off on her bicycle.

"Let's get going," Fiona said after they'd filled up the hay nets. "We need to get the horses back here before it gets dark."

Callie agreed. She locked Tessa in the backyard and checked the house was secure. The windows all worked now, thanks to Noah.

She maneuvered the truck and trailer around the yard and headed for the road.

"So, big date this Friday, huh?"

Callie concentrated on the driving. The trip was close to thirty kilometers west of Bellandale and would take about half an hour. But she still managed to smile at her friend. "How did you find out?"

"Evie told me," Fiona said. "She's watching the kids and asked if I wanted to drop by for a game of rummy." Her friend rolled her eyes. "I get a game of rummy and you get a dreamy date."

Dreamy? She supposed Noah was a little dreamy. *A lot dreamy.* And she was looking forward to their date more than she could have ever imagined. She had only seen him during

Lily's lesson on Sunday because the twins had come down with a slight cold. But he'd asked her to dinner on Friday night. Although after what happened by the river, Callie wasn't sure was ready for the next step in their relationship. Oh, she wanted Noah. What surprised her was the intensity of that desire. She'd never considered herself all that sexual in the past…her life with Craig had revolved around the horses and competition and hard work. Sex and romance had come last in the list of priorities they'd set for their life together.

But with Noah…well, she thought about sex a lot. And she felt certain he thought the same. Since they'd almost made love by the river she'd been distracted and unable to think about much else.

Except now she was thinking about Lily. The young girl's obvious confusion and pain lingered in the back of Callie's mind. She needed to talk with Noah before their relationship went any further. She needed to be sure she wasn't unsettling Lily too much.

"There's the turnoff," Fiona announced.

Callie slowed down and turned into a long gravel driveway. An old farmhouse came into view behind a row of wild bamboo. The settling dusk set up an eerie mood. "Are you sure this is the right place?"

"Absolutely. Put the headlights on, will you? It's getting dark."

Callie flicked on the lights and pulled the truck to a halt. "Looks like a gate over there," she said and pointed to a break in the fence line where an old timber gate was tethered between two posts. Fiona grabbed the flashlight on the seat between them and got out. Callie followed and retrieved three halters and ropes from the back of the truck before tracing her friend's footsteps.

"I can see them," Fiona announced when she reached the fence line. "Look."

Callie saw the three horses silhouetted against the diminishing sunlight. "You get the trailer ready," she said. "I'll grab them."

"Be careful," Fiona warned and headed back to the truck.

Callie looked at the chain and padlocks on the gate and tapped the pair of bolt cutters in her back pocket. She slipped through the barbed-wire fence and headed for the trio of horses who were now watching her suspiciously. The closer she got, the more appalled she became. They were clearly neglected. Two bays and one grey, all of them in need of decent feed and veterinary attention. She haltered one of the bays and the other two automatically followed. Once the three horses were secured, Callie grabbed the snips and cut through the barbed wire. Within minutes they began angle loading them on the trailer.

Fiona suddenly shrieked. "Callie, look. A car's coming."

Sure enough, a pair of headlights turned toward the long driveway. "It could be nothing," Callie assured her friend.

Fiona didn't believe her. She didn't believe herself. "They must have seen our lights. We have to get out of here."

Callie agreed. They quickly secured the horses, closed the tailgate, then jumped into the truck. Callie turned the truck and trailer in a sharp arc and headed down the driveway.

The car kept coming. Conscious of both their own and the horse's safety, Callie accelerated fractionally and stayed on the track. With just meters to spare, the car veered to the right with a loud blast of its horn. She kept going, giving the task her full concentration. Fiona told her the car had turned and was now on their tail as they headed out of the driveway. They hit the main road and Callie increased speed. Behind, the car closed in, tailgating them, striking the horn in an attempt to intimidate. The driver didn't give up, following them down the narrow country road. In the side mirrors Callie could see that the car was in fact a truck with a menacingly heavy-duty push bar out front. And it was getting closer to the back of the trailer with each passing second. At the first contact on the push bar against the rear of the trailer, Callie was thrown forward. Fiona screamed. Callie gripped the steering wheel and held on, managing the impact by pressing the gas and surging forward. She could feel the horses moving in the trailer and straightened the rig quickly. The truck collided again, harder this time, sending them into the gravel rut on the edge of the road. Callie held her nerve and pulled the wheel with all her strength.

"Should we pull over?" Fiona asked frantically.

"No," Callie said quickly. "Cameron's a police officer, right?"

Fiona nodded. "Yeah."

"So, call and tell him where we are and what's happening."

"But he'll—"

"Just call him," she insisted. "Hurry."

Thankfully Fiona had service on her cell and hastily made the call. Cameron instructed them to keep on their route at the designated speed limit if safe and said a police car would be dispatched immediately.

They endured a frightening ten minutes until the welcome sight of blue and red flashing lights came toward them. Callie slowed the truck down and pulled over. The truck took one last ram into the back, jerking them around the cab despite their seat belts. Another police vehicle appeared and cornered the truck behind them.

The offenders were out of their truck within seconds. Two men, hurling insults about how they had stolen their horses, didn't like having to answer questions about how Callie's trailer had dents on the tailgate.

Cameron arrived in plain clothes because he'd been off duty. He was quick to check they were unharmed and asked for a detailed account of what had happened. With the men now in the back of a police car and the horses jittery but in one piece, Callie began to tell her account of the events while Fiona called Animal Welfare to come and pick up the horses. But a sharp rapping sound interrupted them, followed by a shrill voice pleading, "Let me out."

Cameron followed the sound, Callie right behind him. He rattled the handle to the storage compartment on the side of the trailer. Callie quickly gave him the key and he opened the narrow door. None of them expected Lily Preston to unfold her gangly legs from the small space.

"Damn it, Lily," Cameron demanded as he helped her out. "What are you doing in there?"

The teenager straightened, rubbed her arms and looked at Callie. "I just wanted to help."

Callie's blood ran cold. "You stowed away when I told you not to. Lily, how can—"

"Because friends should help each other."

"Does your dad know you're here?" Cameron asked.

Lily shook her head, guilt written all over her face. "Maybe we shouldn't tell him."

Good idea—but not going to happen. Callie watched as Cameron stepped away and made a quick phone call.

By the time Noah received the call from Cameron, he was about to start calling Lily's friends to see if anyone knew where she was. He'd tried Callie several times thinking she'd be there, but she hadn't picked up. Nor could he get any service on her cell. Not surprising, considering Cameron's brief account of events that led to both Lily and Callie ending up at the police station.

He dropped the kids at Evie's and headed into Bellandale. He scored a parking space outside the police station and headed inside. Cameron greeted him swiftly, minus the regulation blue issue uniform.

"Where's Lily?" he demanded.

"In the break room. She's okay," Cameron said.

Relief pitched in his chest. "And Callie?"

"She's just finished making a statement. Room three. You can go in if you like."

Noah strode away without another word. She was sitting down when he entered the room. He said her name.

She looked up, swallowed hard and let out a long, almost agonized sigh. "Noah."

He stepped closer. "Are you all right?"

"Yes, fine."

"What happened?"

She took a deep breath and placed her hands on the small table in front of her. "Fiona and I heard that the three horses we've been trying to rescue had been moved again. We found out the location and went to get them."

"To steal them?"

She raised her hands and stood, scraping the chair back. "Well, yes."

"And what?" he asked, sharper than he wanted. "You thought you'd take my kid along for the ride?"

"No...I had no idea she'd stowed away in the storage locker."

Noah stilled. "She was in the *trailer?*" Cameron hadn't mentioned that.

"Dad?"

They both stopped speaking and turned their heads toward the door. Lily stood beneath the threshold. "Don't blame Callie," his daughter insisted.

"I'm not blaming anyone," he said and tried to stop thinking about the danger his daughter had been in. "I'm trying to understand what happened."

Lily shrugged. "I wanted to help. I wanted to do something. It's not Callie's fault."

"I'm not blaming Callie," he said and tried to push back the kernel of censure rising within his chest. He knew Lily. She was headstrong and impulsive. And Callie couldn't have known his daughter would be so determined to go along for the ride.

"Good," Lily said and raised her chin. "It was *my* fault. I'm the one who should be blamed. It's always my fault. That's what I do."

There was so much pain in Lily's voice that Noah's heart constricted. "Its okay, Lily. Why don't you go and wait by the front desk. We'll go home soon."

Lily looked at them both for a moment then let out a pained breath. "So you can do what? Talk about me and work out ways to get me out of your hair so you two can get it on?"

Noah stepped toward his daughter, but she moved back. "It's not like—"

"Maybe you should send me away somewhere," she said and cut him off. "Like boarding school—that way I won't be in anyone's way. Or maybe you should send me to Paris—you could always ask my mother if she wants me." Lily's eyes glistened with tears Noah knew she wouldn't let fall. "But we know what she'd say, right? She didn't want me four years ago, so she won't want me now."

The pain in his daughter's voice pierced directly into Noah's chest. Lily had kept her feelings about her mother locked away for years. And now they were leaching out. He was staggered and anxious and partly relieved. Realizing why, Noah swallowed a hard lump in his throat. In a matter of weeks Callie had somehow become the catalyst for Lily's stirred emotions.

"You're not going to be sent away, Lily," he assured her gently. "Not ever. Go and wait by the desk. I'll be with you soon."

Before she turned Lily looked toward Callie with eyes filled with apologetic resentment. Noah knew Lily liked and respected Callie, but his daughter was also afraid of the impact Callie was having on their lives.

Once she left Callie spoke. "She's in a lot of pain, Noah."

That much was obvious. "I know."

"She's confused and frightened."

He knew that, too. What he didn't know was why Callie looked at him with such blatant despair. "I'll talk with her."

Callie let out a long sigh. "I don't...I don't think we should do this."

Suddenly Noah knew exactly what she was talking about. And he knew what was coming. She wanted out. Before they'd even begun. It cut right through to the marrow in his bones. Perhaps because part of him knew she was right. Lily's needs had to come first. And whatever his daughter was going through, Noah knew his relationship with Callie would only amplify Lily's feelings of abandonment and anger toward her mother.

But...to lose her? Sensing that it was exactly what Callie wanted made him mad. Irrational and unlike him as it was, Noah experienced a deep burst of resentment for the fact she could give up on them so easily.

"So, I guess you get what you want after all," he said, not liking the way it sounded but too stubborn to stop the words from coming.

"What does that mean?"

"No ready-made family."

Callie looked at him, all eyes, all hurt. "That's unfair. I'm only thinking of Lily. She needs—"

"What about what you need, Callie? Or maybe you don't

need anything. Needing would mean feeling, right?" He pushed past the pain that had settled behind his ribs. "It would mean giving part of yourself to me...and I don't know if you have the heart for it."

She swallowed hard. "Do you think I'm that cold?"

"I don't know," he replied, frustrated and annoyed. "Only you know what's in your heart, Callie."

"I'm trying to do what's best for Lily."

You're what's best for Lily. You're what's best for me.

But he didn't say it. He didn't push. Didn't beg her to give them a chance like he wanted to. "I have to go. I'll see you... sometime."

She lifted her shoulders. "Sure."

Noah left the room. Walking down the corridor suddenly became close to the hardest thing he'd ever done.

Callie sat on the sofa, eating ice cream covered in crushed Oreo cookies and copious amounts of chocolate sauce.

She took a mouthful, anticipating the usual buzz from the sugary sweetness, and sighed heavily when the kick didn't come.

Hopeless.

She tried again and, when disappointed with the same result, plopped the dish on the coffee table and sank back in the sofa. It was Friday night and she was alone. The same Friday night that she should have been out on a romantic date with Noah.

I should be with him right now.

Except that everything was ruined.

Even though she knew there was nothing else she could have done when she realized the extent of Lily's fears, Noah's words had hurt her deeply. She did have a heart capable of feeling. A heart that was filled with thoughts of him.

She hadn't heard from Noah all week. Nor had she seen

Lily. She only had a message on her answering machine telling her he'd decided to take his daughter to Janelle Evans for lessons from now on. Callie had replayed the message countless times, listening for something, some indication he regretted what had happened between them. And because she'd heard nothing like that in the direct, clipped tones, each day dragged out longer than the one before.

She'd tried ignoring the pain suddenly and permanently lodged inside her.

She'd tried not to think about how much she missed him.

And how much she missed Lily. And the rest of his amazing family.

And as she'd thought her heart irreparably broken and imagined she'd never feel anything deep enough to really be hurt ever again, Callie came face-to-face with the truth. And it shocked her to the core.

I love him.

She was in love with Noah.

She wasn't sure how to deal with the feelings that were new, raw and strangely precious. Her head hurt thinking about it. She looked at the melting ice cream and was just about to trade it for some aspirin when Tessa barked and moments later the doorbell rang.

Fiona stood on her doorstep and walked across the threshold holding a bottle of wine in each hand. "We thought we'd come over and cheer you up," her friend announced.

"We?"

Evie Dunn stuck her head around the open door. "She means me." Evie's wildly curling black hair bobbed around her face. "Can I come in?"

"Of course."

Within seconds the door was shut and Fiona scooted to the kitchen for glasses.

"You don't mind?" Evie asked.

Callie shook her head. "I could use the company," she admitted and suggested they take a seat.

Evie sat on the oversize love seat and curled up one foot. "It was Fee's idea."

"I'm glad you're here," Callie said, and tried not to think about how much Evie looked like her brother. And *she* was glad for the company. She had the feeling Evie could become a good friend. She pointed to the bowl on the table and smiled. "I was just about to consume a gallon of ice cream."

"As a substitute for what?" Fiona chirped as she came back into the room.

Callie fought off the embarrassment clinging to her skin and ignored her friend's teasing. "You guys have saved me from a gazillion calories."

Fiona laughed then poured wine into three glasses and passed them around.

"If it's any consolation," Evie said quietly, "he doesn't look any better than you do."

Callie tried not to think about how hearing that made her feel. It wasn't as if either of them had made any kind of declaration to one another. Their relationship had fizzled out before it had really begun. What could she say that wouldn't make her look like a silly, lovesick fool?

"Noah told me some of what happened," Evie said and took a sip of wine. "Lily's pretty broken up that you're not teaching her anymore."

"It's probably for the best."

"I'm not so sure. Sometimes you have to push past the hard times."

"Noah has to focus on Lily," Callie said and took a drink.

Evie tutted. "My brother has focused solely on his kids for the past four years. And apart from Lily's gothic rebellion and typical teenage moodiness, she's never talked about how her mother's departure made her feel. And then wham, you walk into their lives and she starts letting things slip. There's a connection, Callie. Because of you she's opening up and that's a positive thing. Talking about her mother is good for Lily."

"I agree," Callie said. "But she needs to be able to do that without being afraid her world is going to be rocked upside down."

"By you?" Evie asked. "Lily worships you."

Callie's throat tightened. "As *her* friend. Not as…something else."

"You mean Noah's girlfriend? Or a potential stepmother?"

Stepmother? Heavens. How had this happened? How had she become so deeply involved with the Preston's that Evie was suggesting marriage? Loving Noah had changed everything. Not being with him hurt so much Callie wondered how she'd get through it.

"She needs stability," Callie said. "She needs to know her father isn't about to get sidetracked."

"She has stability," Evie said a little more forcibly. "What she needs is to know relationships can work and that not all women are like her mother and will leave her."

Callie agreed. Except she wasn't sure she was the kind of role model Lily needed.

And she suspected Noah thought that, too.

Noah thrummed his fingers on the steering wheel as he waited for Lily. The twins and Jamie, buckled up in the back of the utility vehicle, chatted quietly to one another. Harry was asleep on the front porch. The morning air was warm, typical of a November day. Summer would soon be here. And summer in Crystal Point meant the little township would be buzzing with tourists and convoys of camper trailers and weekend holidaymakers searching for some relief from the unforgiving heat in the clear waters of the surf beach and river mouth. He watched as Lily shut the front door and bolted toward the vehicle. She got into the truck and put on the seat belt.

"Ready to go?" he asked.

"Sure. I hope Maddy's okay."

Maddy Spears had been in a horse-riding accident and her mother Angela had called, asking if he could bring Lily to see her at the hospital.

"I'm sure she'll be fine," Noah assured her and started the engine. "How are the lessons going?" he asked, trying to take her mind off her worrying about her best friend.

Lily rolled her eyes. "I've only had one. And like you don't know that already? I'm sure *she's* told you everything."

She. Janelle Evans. Lily's new instructor. The enemy. Noah hung on to his patience. "I thought you liked Janelle."

She huffed. "You thought wrong. She's so *old.*"

He eased the vehicle into gear. "She's experienced."

Lily's eyes narrowed. "Old," she repeated.

"I think you should cut her some slack," Noah said quietly.

Another huff. "Well, you would. Seeing it was *your* idea that I go there in the first place."

"You said you wanted lessons," Noah reminded her.

"I do. But I don't want them with *her.*" Lily rolled her eyes. "I don't see why I can't go back to Callie. It's not like I broke up with her or anything. I knew I'd be the one who ended up getting screwed."

"Watch the language," he warned.

"At least you're not going to start dating *this* instructor," Lily snapped back. "I mean, she's like one hundred years old or something. So I'm pretty sure you won't marry her."

"Who are you marrying, Daddy?" came a determined voice from the backseat.

Noah spotted Jamie in the rear vision mirror and smiled. "No one, mate."

"You could marry Callie," Jamie said determinedly. "We like her. You like her, too, don't you, Dad?"

"Stupid question," Lily said.

"I'm not stupid," Jamie wailed.

"Yeah, you are."

Noah called a truce. "Stop the name calling." Lily made a face and he suspected Jamie stuck his tongue out in response.

"Are you going to *marry* Callie, Dad?" Jamie asked, almost jumping out of his seat.

Marry Callie? He'd thought about. Imagined it. Wanted it. "Lily and I are only talking."

But Jamie didn't give up. "If you marry Callie she'd be our mother, right?"

"Stepmother," Lily put in.

Jamie ignored his sister. "And would she come to school sometimes and work at the canteen, Dad?"

Noah didn't miss the longing in his son's voice. Such a small thing. But for a little boy who barely remembered a mother's love, it was huge. He'd tried his best, but juggling a business and four kids often made it impossible to do the small things. His sisters pitched in, especially Evie, and his mother did what she could. But it wasn't enough. Who was he kidding? His kids needed a full-time mother.

"Would Callie be our mother, Dad?"

Jamie again, still curious and not put off by Noah's silence. He tried to maintain casualness. "I guess she would."

Lily huffed again, louder this time. "Don't get too excited. We didn't have any luck getting our real mother to hang around. I can't see how Callie would be any different."

Chapter Ten

Callie had no idea that helping Angela Spears select a new pony for her daughter Maddy would end with the teenager taking a tumble from the first horse they looked at. She was relieved that Maddy's broken arm was the worst of her injuries. She had some superficial grazes on her face but none that would scar. The hot pink cast on her arm was finally wrapped and Callie offered to grab coffee for a fraught Angela while the doctor checked the results of a few cautionary tests, including a head scan.

She headed for the cafeteria and purchased coffee for Angela and a soda for Maddy.

When she returned to Maddy's room she saw Lily sitting on the edge of the bed, then saw Jamie and the twins perched together on a single chair and Noah talking closely with Angela.

The green-eyed monster reared its ugly head and she pushed the feeling down as swiftly as she could. A blended family—wasn't that the term used now? Angela was an attractive woman. Noah would be blind not to notice. She was a single mother, he was a single father. A good solution all round—yours, mine and possibly ours one day. Lily and Maddy were best friends. It would be the perfect scenario for Noah's troubled daughter.

And if Callie had any doubts that she'd fallen in love with Noah—they scattered the moment she realized the feeling coursing across her skin was blind, burning jealousy.

She swallowed the bitter taste in her mouth.

Callie placed the coffee on the table beside the bed. The twins rushed toward her and Callie had no hesitation in accepting their warm hug. Jamie quickly did the same. Only Lily hung back. But the teenager looked at her almost hopefully. And Noah's eyes grazed over her, from her feet to the roots of her hair. She felt the energy of his stare, felt her skin heat, felt the tiny hairs on the back of her neck come alive.

Angela's beaming smile didn't help. "Oh, you're back," she said breathlessly. "I was just telling Noah how lucky we were that you were with us today. And it was my fault," Angela wailed. "But it was so hot. I had no idea the pony would spook over a little umbrella."

"It happens sometimes," Callie assured her, fighting her awareness of Noah with all her strength. "Don't feel bad."

"Can we still buy the pony?" Maddy asked, still groggy from painkillers.

Angela looked at Callie. "What do you think?"

Callie smiled and turned to the girl in the bed. "How about we wait until your arm is better and try a few more horses out before making a decision?"

Maddy nodded. "Still…" Her voice trailed. "I'd really like my own horse."

"Me, too," Lily said and looked at her father. "You promised, remember?"

"I remember," he said, still looking at Callie. "We'll see."

Lily rolled her kohl-lined eyes. "Yeah, I know what that means." She looked at her friend. "Now you've busted your arm I haven't a chance."

Angela came across the room and hugged Callie. "Thank you for everything," she said, her eyes clogged with emotion. "If you hadn't been there, I don't know what I would have done. I wouldn't have known how to splint her arm like that. And the way you knew to keep her warm in case she went into shock." She shuddered. "I wouldn't have remembered any of that."

"I'm glad I could help."

"Help?" Angela hugged her again. "You were incredible. I'm hopeless in a crisis."

"Not hopeless," Callie said gently. "And I have to know basic first aid as part of my license to teach."

"It didn't look basic to me. Anyway, I'm so grateful you were there."

"Well, I'll get going." She looked quickly around the room, focusing on Angela. "Are you sure your sister will be coming to pick you up?"

"Oh, yes," the other woman replied. "You go, please. You've done more than enough. And thank you for coming here with us. I know it helped Maddy enormously knowing you were by her side."

She said goodbye to the kids and then turned without another word, pain slicing through her with every step she took. She made it about thirty feet down the corridor when she heard Noah saying her name. *I will not look back. I will not let him see how much I miss him.*

"Callie, wait up."

That stopped her. She inhaled deeply and turned to face him. "What?"

"Are you okay?"

Can't you see that I'm not? Can't you see that I'm crazy in love with you? But I can't come between your family. I won't.

"Why wouldn't I be?"

He looked into her eyes. "You had a fairly harrowing afternoon."

"I handled it."

"So Angela said."

Angela. Perfect single mother Angela. "Is there something else you want?" she asked and couldn't believe the sound of her own voice.

"Maddy's lucky you were there."

Callie felt prickles of annoyance weave up her spine. "I guess I have my uses."

He felt the sting of her response because he expelled an almost weary breath. "I just wanted to say…that it's…it's good to see you."

"I have to go," she said quickly and pulled her keys from her pocket. "I've got a student this afternoon," she lied.

He went to say something and then stopped. "Yeah, sure."

Her heart felt like it was going to burst. *I will not fall apart in front of him.* "Goodbye, Noah."

She turned before he could say anything and walked purposefully down the corridor.

By the time she'd returned to Sandhills Farm it was nearly two o'clock. Joe was there, wheeling a barrow of soiled manure from the stables when she pulled up. He asked about Maddy and she gave him a condensed version of what had happened.

"Saddle up Indy for me, will you?" she asked. "The Western saddle please. I'm going for a long ride."

Callie rode toward Crystal Point, through the cane fields, past sweet potato farmers cultivating their crops. She rode past the local primary school, took a trail toward the river and lingered by the boat ramp for a while, eating the sandwich and water she'd packed in her saddle bag while Indy happily grazed on Rhodes grass.

I'm such a fool. For years she'd frozen herself off from feeling anything. And then along came Noah and his incredible kids and suddenly she felt like she was *all* feelings. All want. All need. But she hurt, too. And she didn't know how to stop the hurt…or how to stop loving Noah.

It was past five when she returned home, and it was an hour later when she headed for the house after strapping Indy down, returning her tack to the stables and locking the gelding into his stall. By seven o'clock, once the animals were all fed and bedded down for the night, Callie had showered, put on a pair of sweats and sat on the sofa with her laptop to check her email. One from her brother, Scott, made her smile and she was just about to hit the reply button when she heard a car pull up outside.

He's here.

She knew it somehow. Felt it deep down. Tessa barked and Callie quickly made her way to the front door and flicked on the porch light. She opened the door.

It *was* Noah.

He stood beneath the light. "Hey." He looked so good in jeans and a white golf shirt. Her heart lurched in her chest. "I probably should have called first."

Callie crossed her arms, determined to be strong. "Why didn't you?"

"I thought you might hang up." He ran his hand through his hair. "Can we talk?"

She opened the screen door and waited until he'd crossed the threshold before closing both doors. "What did you want to talk about?" she asked once they'd moved into the living room.

He cleared his throat. "I wanted to…I wanted…"

Callie didn't move as she pushed her emotions down. "What?"

He let out an exasperated breath. "I don't really know. I let Lily stay with Maddy, and after I left the hospital I dropped the kids off at my parents. For the past two hours I've been driving around, thinking, trying to get things right in my head."

"What things?" she asked quietly.

He swallowed. "Us. The kids. Why I can't stop thinking about you."

Callie's knees gave up and she sat on the edge of the sofa. "It's the same for me," she admitted.

He came forward and stood a couple of feet from her. "So, what are we going to do about it?"

Callie shrugged. "Nothing's changed, Noah."

"You're right about that."

"You'd really be better off with someone else," she heard herself say. Stupid words. Words to cover the feelings coursing through her blood.

"Someone else?"

She shrugged. "Like Angela," she said, although her voice cracked and she knew he'd heard it. "She's a single parent, she obviously loves kids—she'd make you a good match."

"I'm not interested in Angela Spears," he said quietly.

"But Lily—"

"Tell me what *you* want, Callie."

"How can it matter, Noah? Last week you—"

"Last week I said something stupid and hurtful. And I'm sorry. I told you once that I'd never hurt you. But you were about to blow me off and I got mad and screwed up." He shrugged his shoulders tightly. "Can you forgive me?"

Callie nodded. "But it doesn't change anything. Someone like Angela would fit into your life. And with Lily and Maddy being friends it makes perfect sense."

"Not to me. I'm interested in you, Callie. I *want* you. Only you."

"But Lily—"

"Will be fine with this. With *us*. I know my daughter. And I know how she feels about you."

Callie wasn't so sure. She knew the teenager was confused and at a critical point in her young life. Callie didn't want to do anything to jeopardize the young girls well-being.

"If she doesn't…" Callie's word trailed.

"She will understand."

He stood in front of her, not moving, not speaking. Just looking at her from bright-green eyes. Finally, when neither could bear the silence any longer, he dropped to his knees in front of her and wrapped his arms around her.

He shuddered in her arms. "I can hardly breathe just thinking about you."

She wanted to deny him. She wanted to refuse the clamoring needs of her body and the deep longing in her heart. But refusing him, rejecting him, would break her into tiny pieces.

I love this man…

Callie ran her hands through his hair. "Me, too."

The air suddenly filled with heat. And need. She could feel the mounting tension in him beneath her hands. His muscles tightened and she instinctively gripped him harder. Warmth spread through her body, licking over every nerve, every cell. She knew he felt it, too. It rolled like waves, creating a turbulent energy in the quiet room.

Callie's hands slid down his arms, over strong biceps. She rubbed his skin with her thumbs and heard the unsteady sound of his breathing.

"Callie," he said, drawing the words deep from his throat. "I want…I want to make love to you." He stilled, taking in a profound breath. "But if you're not ready...we'll wait. And if you want me to go I—"

She smiled. "Shhhh." She traced her hands back to his shoulders. He felt so strong. *I can have this...I can have him.* "I'm glad you're here," she whispered. "I want you here. I think I've wanted you here my whole life."

Noah immediately moved closer, fisting a handful of her hair before he tilted her head back and took her mouth in a searing, hungry kiss. She met his tongue, felt the warm slide of it against the roof her mouth, and then tangled her own around his. His arms tightened around her and slid down her back, cradling her hips and then farther, curving possessively under her bottom. Callie arched forward and wrapped her legs around his hips. She pressed into him, all need, all want. She felt him hard against her and a rush of warmth pooled between her thighs.

"Where's your bedroom?" he muttered against her lips.

"Down the hall, first door on the left."

He kissed her again and stood up, lifting her with effortless strength, and strode down the hallway, shouldering the door open. The small lamp cast shadows around the room and created a welcoming intimacy. Noah placed her on the bed as though she were a fragile doll, flipped off his shoes, shucked off his shirt and lay down beside her.

He kissed her again, her lips, her throat, her neck, and dispensed with the four buttons holding her top together. His eyes glittered when he saw the white lace bra.

"You are lovely," he said, tracing a finger up and over the generous swell of cleavage.

She moved to her knees and slowly inched down the sweat bottoms, dispensing them to the floor. He looked at her with open desire and ran one finger from the top of her neck to the base of her spine, touching the edge of her briefs.

"A tattoo?"

The winged horse looked majestic in flight and Noah moaned his approval as he reached for her and coaxed her to lie beside him. He kissed her again, long and slow, branding her with his kisses, making her his own. He cupped her breasts and gently caressed them. His tongue trailed across her skin, brushing across the edge of the lace. Her nipples ached for his touch, the feel of his mouth, his tongue.

"Take it off," she begged. "Please."

He did so with remarkable efficiency, flicking the hooks at the back with his thumb.

"You've done that before," she breathed.

He chuckled. "Not for a *very* long time," he said as he chucked the bra to the floor and his mouth closed over one straining nipple.

Callie felt the pleasure of it through to her feet. She gripped his shoulders, wanting more, needing more. It was like nothing on earth. His breath was hot against the hardened peak as he suckled. He placed his leg between hers and Callie bucked against him. Pleasure ricocheted over every nerve ending as the abrasive denim he wore rubbed against her sex. She reached down to touch him, felt him shudder as her hand slid across the hardness of his erection straining against his jeans. Her hand moved up, over the zipper, to the belt and she pulled the leather strap free and flicked the top button. Her fingers played with the silky hair arrowing downward.

He groaned and kissed her again, taking her mouth with such hot, scorching possession Callie arched her back, straining off the bed. His hand moved over her skin, her shoulders, her hip and across her belly, then dipped below the tiny triangle of fabric covering her. She felt an intense pleasure as his fingers sought access between the sweet, wet folds and found the tiny nub waiting for his touch.

"Oh, Noah."

He touched her, softly at first, finding the rhythm she liked. She was so wet and welcoming he was surprised he was able to control himself. But he took a deep breath, and another, in between kissing her beautiful mouth. He wasn't going to rush loving her, no matter how badly his body wanted release. He had lips to kiss, breasts to worship, skin to touch and taste. Things he dreamed of doing since the first time he'd met her.

And he would. All night and into the morning.

She moved beneath the pressure of his hand, spreading her thighs trustingly, saying his name over and over. Noah thought he might explode. He felt her tense, heard the change in her breathing, felt her stiffen, waiting, climbing. His aching arousal pushed against his pants. She rocked against the pressure of his hand and he cupped her, then released, then cupped her again. He felt the pulse of her orgasm through his fingertips, saw her skin flush with pleasure and heard her earthy moans of satisfaction.

Desire for her washed over him; love for her filled every cell, every ounce of his blood, and every inch of his skin. He kissed her again—wild, needy kisses that she returned.

"I've never…" she whispered. "Amazing."

Noah dragged the briefs over her thighs, suddenly impatient to see her, marveling at how beautiful she was. He licked her breasts, her rib cage, her belly and lower. He kissed her gently, exploring the soft, moist flesh with his tongue, tasting the sweet musky scent that was uniquely hers. She was incredibly responsive, moaning her pleasure. Her hands gripped his shoulders as he continued his erotic kiss. When he trailed his lips back up across her stomach she writhed beneath him.

He was so hungry for her, so desperate to lose himself inside her, his entire body shook. She held on—his shoulders, his back, his waist.

When her hands hung from his belt, she whispered. "You're wearing too many clothes."

Noah got rid of his jeans and briefs in seconds and returned to her side.

She touched him, enclosing her fingers around his erection and he almost jumped out of his skin.

It's been too long since I've done this...

He took a deep breath and filled his lungs with air. Her touch was gentle, almost uncertain. Noah covered her hand with his and whispered encouragement. She didn't need much. She caressed him from the tip to the base, slowly, building a steady rhythm, driving him crazy with need. All he could think of was Callie—of this beautiful woman who held him, touched him, kissed him back with so much passion he felt truly humbled.

He took a moment and withdrew a foil packet from his wallet. She took the condom, her hands unsteady as she sheathed him. He let her do it and when the pressure became too much, when the need to be inside her drew the breath from his throat in a ragged groan, Noah moved over her. He kissed her and she parted her thighs. He entered her slowly, kissing her more, mimicking the movement of his body as she accepted him inside her

She moved, stretching to take him in, wriggling in a deliciously sexy way. Finally, he was home, filling her, more a part of her than he'd ever been of anyone.

There would never be a moment like this again...their first time...he'd remember the feeling for the rest of his life.

Noah rested his weight on his elbows and looked into her face. She smiled. He touched her hair, remembering how it was one of the first things he'd noticed about her. Such beautiful, luscious hair fanned around the pillow. He kissed her, glorious hot kisses she returned. When he moved against her she moaned, meeting his movements, matching the steady rhythm building between them. All he could feel was Callie, her heat, her wetness surrounding him, enslaving him. He heard her soft cries of pleasure, almost felt them through to his soul as her body arched and shuddered beneath him.

And finally, when the pressure built until he couldn't hold off any longer, it claimed him with white-hot fury, taking him over the edge, ripping through him with the sheer intensity and power of release.

"I love you, Callie." He breathed the words, feeling them with every fiber inside him.

Callie waited until Noah withdrew from her and fell back against the pillow before she took a breath.

I love you...

He'd said the words. It could have been an impulse, a sex-induced moment of euphoria where anything goes. A kind of mid-orgasmic madness. But Callie doubted it. Noah wasn't the kind of man who did anything by half-measures.

He loves me.

He took her hand and kissed her knuckles. "Are you okay?"

I'm out of my mind.

"Oh, yes."

He grinned and closed his eyes. "You're so beautiful."

She felt beautiful. She felt wholly desired and so completely pleasured all she could think of was experiencing it again and again. Callie touched his chest and felt him tense as she played with one flat nipple, then the other. She leaned forward and licked the spot and smiled as the small bud peaked beneath the gentle flick of her tongue. He lay perfectly still and for a moment she thought he'd fallen asleep. But, no—he was smiling, taking long breaths, letting her explore. She kissed his shoulder, nipping at his skin with her teeth before licking the spot. She ran her hand down his stomach and lingered at his belly button, playing with the soft hair trailing downward. When her finger inched lower he quickly covered her hand with his.

"Give me a couple of hours, okay?"

Callie maneuvered her hand from his and grazed her knuckles over him. "I'll give you an hour."

As it turned out he only needed forty minutes. Then Noah made love to her again. He teased her, taunted her with his mouth and tongue and finally, when she thought she could stand no more, he flipped over and dragged her on top. He held her hips, allowing her to ease her body onto his, taking him in, sheathing him inside her. Callie felt wild and wanton as she rode above him. He linked her fingers through his and he supported her weight as she moved, slowly at first, savoring each delicious slide. Then he pulled her forward and sucked her nipples every time her breasts bounced near his mouth. She flung her head back, driving harder, feeling the pressure build and calling his name as pleasure flooded every cell. He lifted off the bed as his climax ripped through him and Callie clenched her internal muscles, taking everything, giving everything, loving him more in that moment than she'd ever imagined she could love anyone.

Spent, they lay together, legs entwined. After a while she rolled onto her stomach and he fingered the tattoo at the base of her spine.

"Do you have any idea how sexy that is?" he said, kissing her shoulder.

"Uh, no. How?"

Callie felt his breath against her skin. "Shall I show you?"

She curled her fingers through the dark smatter of hair on his chest. "Absolutely."

They lingered in bed for another half hour then took a shower together. Afterward Callie made roast beef and mustard sandwiches and they sat in front of the television and watched a rerun of David Letterman.

By midnight they were back in bed, lying on their sides, facing one another.

"So," she said, touching his face. "You're staying?"

He frowned. "Of course."

Callie closed her eyes, feeling safe, feeling loved.

Waking up beside the man who loved you really was the most wonderful way to start a new day. Especially when that man roused you with a trail of kisses along your shoulder blade.

"Good morning," he said softly, slanting his mouth over hers.

Callie smiled against his lips. "Yes, it is."

"What are your plans for today?" he asked, moving from her mouth to her jaw and then to the sensitive spot below her earlobe.

"Oh, the usual," she said on a dreamy sigh. "Well, I used to have a student at eight o'clock."

"Used to?"

"She's with someone else now."

He smiled. "Actually, that's not working out so well."

"Oh. Why not?"

"Lily wants what she wants," he replied, still kissing her. "And she wants you."

"Janelle's a good teacher."

"Not as good as you," he countered. "Then again, I don't imagine anyone is."

Callie heard the lovely compliment and sighed contentedly. "Bring her back next week."

"She'd like that," he said.

"Good. What about you?" she asked. "What are your plans?"

"I've got to pick the kids up this morning. Do you feel like doing something later?"

Callie ran her hand down his chest and lower, lingering past his belly. "What did you have in mind?"

"The beach?"

Callie's hand stilled. "You mean...all together?" A family day out, that's what he meant. *I'm not ready for that yet.*

"That was the idea."

She shifted across the bed and grabbed her gown. "We'll see what happens." She stood up and slipped efficiently into the wrap. "How about breakfast?"

Fifteen minutes later Noah emerged from the shower, dressed and sporting an incredibly sexy shadow of beard on his face. When he entered the kitchen she passed him coffee and a plate topped with some kind of charred-looking bread.

"What's that?" he asked, looking at the contents on the plate.

"Toasted bagel."

He didn't look convinced. "Okay." He sat down, grabbed the toast and took a bite. "You were right," he said easily. "You can't cook."

Callie smiled. "Told ya."

He put down the toast and looked at her. "Are you okay?"

She shrugged and turned toward the countertop. "Of course."

"No regrets?"

Callie shook her head. She had no regrets about making love with him. "No."

"You look far away."

She swallowed, wondering when he'd gotten to know her so well. "I'm right here. Promise."

He drank his coffee and then stood. "I have to get going," he said when he reached her. He turned her in his arms. "But I'll call you later."

"I'd like that."

He kissed her softly and ran his hands over her hips. "I'll let myself out."

She nodded. "Okay."

Noah kissed her again and Callie didn't let out her breath until she heard the soft click of the front screen door closing behind him.

So, what now? She didn't have a clue. He'd said he loved her and she hadn't said it back.

And pretty soon, Callie was certain, he would want to know why not.

Chapter Eleven

Something was wrong. Noah felt it, sensed it. As he drove to his parents' house to pick up the kids he couldn't get the thought out of his mind. She'd retreated. She'd pulled back into a place he couldn't reach. The passionate woman he'd made love with had been absorbed by the woman he remembered from weeks earlier. The woman who didn't want to get involved.

Did she regret it? Was that it? She'd said no. But how could he be sure?

Noah certainly wasn't about to regret the most incredible sex he'd ever had. Because it was more than that. More than sex. Just…more. More everything. More in a way he'd never imagined possible. Touching Callie, loving her, waking up beside her had filled the empty place he'd had inside him for so long.

But the niggling thought stayed with him.

I said I love you. And she didn't say it back.

He'd felt it. In her touch, her sighs, the tears shining in her blue eyes. But, as much as he tried to convince himself it didn't matter, he knew he wanted the words.

He *needed* the words.

When he pulled into the driveway of his parents' home he saw Evie's car outside. His sister was in the kitchen, baking alongside their mother, while the twins and Jamie were in the backyard tormenting his father with a game of Twister.

His mother and sister smiled when he entered the room and then looked at each other.

"Hi. The kids are out the back," Evie said, elbow deep in a large bowl of dough. "Poor Dad," she said with a laugh.

When M.J. trounced into the room moments later, Noah felt the full scrutiny of three sets of curious female eyes.

"Is that a hickey on your neck?" M.J. asked with straight-faced innocence.

Noah's hand instinctively went to his throat.

"Gotcha," M.J. laughed.

"You should never have been taught how to speak," he said quietly, removing his hand and trying not to look self-conscious.

"So, are there wedding bells in the air?" M.J. asked with a big grin.

He scowled. "Watch yourself, kid."

"We have it on good authority."

Noah looked at M.J. and then his mother and Evie.

"Jamie said something this morning," Evie explained. "He's quite excited about the idea."

Noah remembered the conversation he'd had in the truck with the kids. He turned to his mother. "Thanks for watching them."

"How's Maddy?" Evie asked, still digging into dough.

"Broken arm."

"She's lucky Callie was there," Evie said. "Lily called and told us what happened."

He nodded. "Quite the hotline you girls have going."

"Well you never tell us anything," M.J. complained.

Nor did he intend to. "With good reason," he quipped. "Thanks again," he said to his mother, Barbara, who patted his shoulder affectionately.

It took ten minutes to finish saying goodbye and load the kids in the truck. Noah collected Lily on the way home, declining Angela's offer for coffee. When he got home he called Callie, amused by his own eagerness. She answered her cell on the seventh ring and he wondered if she'd considered not picking up. She sounded friendly enough and they talked for a while. She told him she had a new student that afternoon and would have to take a rain check on his idea for the beach.

Noah didn't push the idea. He ended the call with an invitation to his parents' home for the coming Saturday. But instinct told him something was wrong.

Callie knew Noah felt her pull back. And she knew she was acting like a first-rate coward. One mention of his kids and she'd panicked. It wasn't remotely rational. But since when was fear ever rational?

The kids were part of him. His blood. His life.

If she wanted Noah—and she did—then she had to learn how to deal with the reality of his children. She had to love them with her whole heart.

And without really understanding why, her heart simply didn't feel big enough for all that love. It was something she needed to talk to him about. He was smart. If he hadn't figured it out already, he would soon enough. He'd sensed something was wrong, and Callie knew if they had any chance of a future together they needed complete honesty between them.

But she put it off.

On Saturday night they were going to his parents' home for an anniversary party.

She waited on the porch for him to collect her while counting bugs brave enough to aim flight at the mosquito zapper hung from the ceiling. She was nervous about meeting his family. Foolish, she supposed. She already knew Evie, and M.J. and Cameron and she suspected his parents were good people—they would have to be to have raised such a son.

He arrived on time and her stomach did a silly roll when he got out of the truck. He looked great in dark cargo pants and a polo shirt. Her heart crunched up. The kids were in the backseat, she noticed, minus Lily, and she wondered if that was why he didn't kiss her.

"You look beautiful," he said as she got into his vehicle.

Callie smiled and looked in the back, and the three younger children greeted her with a chorus of hellos. They were clearly excited to see her. Shame licked along her spine. They were great kids. And they genuinely cared for her.

I just have to let myself love them without guilt. Without feeling like I'm letting go of Ryan.

Because *that* was what she was afraid of. Losing Ryan. Forgetting Ryan. Replacing Ryan.

"Where's Lily?" she asked, pushing the idea aside for the moment. She'd concentrate on the present and enjoy the moment. There was time for thoughts later.

"With Evie," he replied. "They're meeting us there."

He drove into Crystal Point and pulled up outside a large, two-story home one street back from The Parade in a quiet cul-de-sac. The gardens were immaculate; the home looked like it was made for a large family. A couple of cars were parked in the driveway and he pulled up off the curb.

The moment she walked into their home, Barbara and Bill Preston greeted her with smiles and a warm welcome. Barbara hugged her son closely and Callie didn't miss the gentle way she ruffled his hair and smiled at him, like they had a lovely secret between them. The twins and Jamie clearly adored their grandparents and were rustled away with their grandfather to play a game of Wii bowling before the guests began to arrive.

"The girls are in the kitchen," Barbara said. "Join us after you've shown Callie the house."

Callie followed when Noah led her upstairs.

"So," she said, standing in the middle of a room at the top of the stairway. "This was your bedroom when you were growing up?"

He smiled. "Yep."

It appeared to be as typical a teenage boy's room as you'd get. Blue quilt and accessories, shelves filled with trophies, faded posters of rock bands on the walls. She took a closer look at the trophies—some for sports, some for academics.

"So you were a jock?" she asked, picking up a medal awarded for a code of football she'd vaguely heard of. She fingered another one granted for rowing. "Looks like you were good at it." She placed the medal down. "How old were you when you moved out?"

"Eighteen," he said. "I moved to Brisbane to study engineering."

"Is that where you met your wife?"

He took a step toward her. "Ex-wife," he corrected. "And no. I always knew I'd take the business over from my father, but I wanted to experience life a bit before I came back to Crystal Point." He picked an old volleyball off the floor and tossed it onto the narrow bed. "I finished my degree in three years, then took off. I backpacked in Europe for about a year, until my money ran out. Then I worked at a pub in London trying to save enough for my fare back home, which is where I met Margaret. She was there on a dancing scholarship. We hooked up and I stayed for another year or so. But I always intended to come back." He shrugged. "A couple of months after I got home she called to say she was pregnant."

"And then you married her?" She hoped he didn't hear the tinge of jealousy in her tone.

He reached for her. "Let's not talk about that, okay?" His arms tightened around her. "I'd much rather kiss you."

And he did. So thoroughly Callie thought she might pass out.

When they returned downstairs the kitchen was a hive of activity. Mary-Jayne was there decorating a cheesecake, and Evie was wrapping potatoes in aluminum foil.

Both sisters' eyes popped wide when they saw them, but to their credit they didn't say anything. Lily was there, glaring at Callie with confused eyes. The teenager headed to the living room and mumbled something about how it was "typical" and no one cared what she wanted.

"Should I go and talk with her?" Callie asked.

Noah shook his head. "She'll be fine."

"He's right," Evie said. "She's just reacting. Lily doesn't know how she's feeling."

"All teenagers are obnoxious," Mary-Jayne announced. "Remember how I was?"

Noah smiled. "Was?"

Everyone laughed and Callie was struck by the deep affection they shared for one another. It made her miss her own family.

Within half an hour the celebration had taken itself outside. The outdoor entertainment area was huge and had been transformed with a long buffet table and chairs for those inclined to sit. Music filtered through strategically placed speakers. People started arriving, including Cameron Jakowski and Fiona, who were both well acquainted with the Prestons. He shook Noah's hand, kissed Barbara on the cheek while steal-

ing a piece of cheese off a plate and teased M.J. about her
Don't Blame Me...I Voted For The Other Guy apron.

Fiona gave Callie an unexpected hug. "I'm glad you're
here," she whispered. She grabbed Callie's arm and pulled
her aside. "So you're really dating now?" Fiona asked in a
ludicrously excited voice.

Dating? They were lovers—did that count as dating?
"We're...something."

She looked across the deck to where Noah stood with
Cameron—and also the most beautiful woman Callie had
ever seen, decked out in what was clearly a high-end designer
dress of deep red and incredible four-inch heels. "Who's
that?" she asked.

Fiona looked up and her pretty face turned into a grimace.
"Princess Grace."

"Huh?'

"Noah's sister," she explained. "She's some hot-shot busi-
nesswoman in New York. A real cold fish. You can freeze ice
on her—"

"I get the picture." Callie smiled. "She's stunning."

Fiona made a face. "Yeah, yeah. Beautiful and about as
pleasant as global warming."

Callie's eyes widened. "Would your opinion have anything
to do with the fact she's talking to Cameron right now?"

Fiona blushed. "No point," she admitted. "We're destined
to be *just friends.*"

Callie sensed the disappointment in her friend's voice.
"There's someone out there for you."

Fiona raised both her brows. "Spoken like a woman who's
fallen in love."

Callie froze when she felt a strong arm unexpectedly
moved around her waist. She looked at Fiona and her friend's
eyes popped wide open.

Had he heard Fiona's teasing?

She felt his breath in her ear. "Dance with me?"

She pulled back. "Dance where?"

"By the pool," he said.

Callie looked toward the pool area. Strategically placed candles created a soft, romantic mood and she couldn't resist joining the few couples already swaying to the music. "Okay."

Moments later she was in his arms. His parents were there, she noticed, dancing cheek to cheek and clearly still in love after many years of marriage.

"What are you thinking?" he asked.

"That your parents look happy together."

Noah smiled. "They make it look easy."

She looked at him, conscious of how close they were as he kissed her forehead gently. She could feel his thighs against her own every time they moved and a jolt of need arrowed low in her belly.

She knew what he read in her eyes, knew he could feel it in the vibration coming off her skin. "Ah, Callie," he said, so close to her ear his mouth was against the lobe. He kissed the sensitive spot. "I want to take you home and make love to you."

"I want that, too," she breathed.

"In my bed?" he queried.

His bed? Somewhere they hadn't ventured. "I'm not…"

"Not ready for that?"

Callie sighed. "I want us to be close, Noah. Really, I do."

"As what? Lovers?"

They were lovers. And she wanted to make love with him again. But she knew that for Noah that wouldn't be enough. "Yes…for now."

"We're going to have to talk about the future at some—"

"I know," she said quickly and pressed closer. *But later,* she thought cowardly.

For the moment she wanted to enjoy the dance, the moment, the knowledge that she was safe in his arms. She rested her head against his shoulder.

"Callie?"

"Mmm," she murmured, inhaling the scent of him, the mixtures of some citrusy shampoo and masculine soap.

"What Fiona said…is it true?"

So he had heard?

Callie's gaze dropped. "I…feel it."

"But you can't say it?" If he was frustrated by her response, he didn't show it. He rubbed her cheek with his thumb. "One day, maybe?"

She nodded, her head and heart pounding.

"One day," she said on a breath. "I promise."

Becoming lovers changed everything. With complete intimacy came vulnerability. Noah was an incredible lover—caring, unselfish and delightfully energetic. But despite all that, Callie felt the wedge growing between them, gaining momentum. *It's of my own making.* And she was positive Noah could feel it, too.

He didn't say a word. But he was on edge. Like he was waiting, anticipating.

He's waiting for me to say something. He's waiting for me to say "I love you…" or "I can't be with you…"

Four days later she still felt it, even as she rolled over, caught up in a tangle of limbs and sighed with a mix of pleasure and utter exhaustion.

It was light inside her bedroom, despite the thick curtains being drawn. The sun peeked through, teasing her, making her feel just that little bit wicked. Speaking of wicked, she thought, running lazy fingers through the hair on Noah's chest, which was still rising and falling as he took in deep breaths. He had such a wickedly good body…

"You know," he said between breaths. "I really can't keep taking time off during the day." He smiled. "Not that this isn't a great way to spend the afternoon."

She fingered one flat nipple. "Mmm...great."

"I've got a business to run."

The nipple pebbled. "Mmm...I know."

"My staff will start wondering why I'm leaving every afternoon."

She trailed her fingertips downward. "You could tell them it's a long lunch."

He smiled. "Speaking of lunch, we should probably eat something."

"Food for energy, hey?" Callie wriggled and rolled toward him. "Am I working you too hard?" she asked, smiling and kissing his rib cage.

Noah reached for her chin and tilted her face upward. "I'm not one of your horses you have to exercise to keep in shape."

Callie pulled herself up and lay on top of him. "No, you're not. I mean, I do love my horses..." She trailed kisses across his jaw. "But you're...I mean I'm..." The words got lost.

Noah cupped her cheek and made her look at him. "Don't backpedal now."

For the past three days they'd spent each afternoon in bed together. Callie couldn't get enough of him. She couldn't feel him enough, kiss him enough and love him enough. But she knew it was a fantasy. A fabulous fantasy—but still a fantasy. Being lovers, uninterrupted by the realities of life, wasn't sustainable.

They *had* to talk. About their future. About his children. About Lily.

About Ryan.

"Are you free Friday night?" he asked instead. "I thought you could come over and let me cook for you. What do you say?"

"I have a competition on Saturday," she replied. "And Fiona's staying over Friday night so we can get an early start."

"Right. What about Saturday night?"

She moved, shifting off him. "I'll probably be quite tired. Can I see how I feel after the comp?"

He sat up and draped the sheet over his legs. "Sure. And Sunday?"

"Lily's having a lesson Sunday."

Callie averted her eyes, trying not to get distracted by his chest as she slipped out of bed. She felt completely comfortable walking naked around the room and liked the way he admired her as she retrieved her clothes from the floor. She looked at the clock on the bedside table. It was three-thirty. "We should get moving. I have a student at four o'clock. And Lily—"

"Usually comes here Wednesdays," he said when she hesitated. "Yes, I know."

"Well I wouldn't want her to see you...see us..."

Noah frowned and pushed back the bedclothes. "She knows about us, Callie. I took you to meet my parents...she also knows I wouldn't do that unless we were serious."

"I just—"

"At least, *I'm* serious," he said, cutting her off. "You—I'm not so sure."

Callie inhaled a shaky breath. "Of course I'm serious. I just don't want to upset Lily."

Noah reached for his clothes, which were still on the floor. "Lily will have to get used to it." He pulled on his briefs and chinos and started adjusting his belt but then stopped. He looked at her. "You know, Callie, Lily is precious to me... but she doesn't get to decide who I fall in love with."

Callie's blood stilled. Her eyes never left his face. "Can't we just keep a low profile for a while?" she asked quietly and grabbed an elastic band off the dresser to tie up her hair.

He shrugged. "I won't hide our relationship from my kids."

Callie took a deep breath. "I'm only asking for a little time."

"It sounds like you're asking me to lie to my children."

She didn't like the accusation and quickly gave him a look that said so. "That's not what I want. But please just respect my wishes."

"As you respect mine?"

"That's not fair."

Noah pulled his shirt over his shoulders. "Neither is making me feel as though you're not in this for the long haul."

"Because I want to take things slowly?"

He grabbed his keys from the bedside table. "Slowly? Ripping one another's clothes off every time we're together isn't exactly slow, Callie." Noah grabbed his shoes and sat on the edge of the bed to put them on. When he was done he stood, turned and faced her. "It's pretty clear you don't want to spend time with the kids," he said quietly.

She shook her head, wanting to deny it because it sounded so incredibly callous.

"I can see in your eyes that you want to negotiate," he said. "And if I loved you less, Callie...maybe I could."

"Noah, I—"

"I've been hammered in the past," he said quietly and came around the bed. "And honestly, I didn't think I'd ever want to take a chance at feeling this way. I didn't think I'd ever want to share my life with someone again...or trust someone...or maybe get married again. But if I learned anything from those years with my ex-wife, it was that I intend on living the rest of my life true to myself. That's what I'm trying to do here." He took a deep breath. "And I can't be your lover if that's all it's ever going to be."

Callie couldn't move. "I don't know what to say to you."

He stood barely feet in front of her. "Well, when you figure it out, maybe you can let me know."

"Don't leave like this," she said shakily. "Not after we've..." She looked at the bed and the rumpled bedclothes.

"Sex isn't enough for me," he said. "Not even incredible sex." He rattled his keys impatiently. "I told you I couldn't and wouldn't enter into something casual. My kids deserve better...and frankly, so do I." He headed for the door and once there, turned back to face her. "And, Callie, so do you."

It took about thirty seconds for her feet to work. By then she'd already heard the front door close.

I'm losing him.

So do something.

Callie pushed determination into her legs and followed him. When she swung the front screen door wide she saw two things—Lily's bicycle left haphazardly at the bottom of the stairs and Lily standing by the bottom step, glaring up at her father who stood on the porch.

She looked like thunder. "Great," she said when she saw Callie. "This is just great."

"It's nothing to do with you, Lily," Noah said quietly.

"Ha." She rolled her green eyes. "It will be when it turns to crap. Adults can't get anything right." She crossed her arms. "It always turns to crap. Always. Look at Maddy's stepfather. And my mother." She made a pained, huffing sound. "She didn't hang around." She gave Callie a searing, accusing look. "And this will be the same."

Callie wanted to assure the teenager that it wouldn't. But the words got stranded on the end of her tongue.

"How about you move your bike to the truck and I'll take you home?" Noah said.

Lily's mouth pursed. "I came to see Samson," she said hotly. "See—it's starting already. You guys had a fight and now I have to do what you want."

"We haven't fought," Callie heard herself deny.

Lily's brows snapped up. "Yeah, right." She pointed to her father. "He comes out and slams the door and you come out after. That's a fight. I'm not a little kid, you know. So go ahead and fight—see if I care."

She turned around and raced toward the stables. Noah took the steps to go after her but Callie called him back.

"Let me go," Callie offered. "I'll talk with her. You know, girl to woman." She pulled on her boots near the door and headed toward the stables.

Callie found Lily by the fence in the yard behind the stables. Samson was with her, butting his whiskery chin against Lily's hand as he searched for morsels of carrot. As she watched them together she saw the bond forming between the teenager and the lovable gelding. It made her remember the early days of her relationship with Indiana and how sixteen years later they were still together.

"He's very attached to you," she said to Lily as she approached.

Lily shrugged. "He's a good horse." She stroked his neck. "Maybe I'll get to have a horse of my own one day."

Callie reached the fence and laid one boot on the bottom rung. "I'm sure you will. Lily, about your dad and me. I want to explain—"

"I think my dad loves you," Lily said unexpectedly.

Callie blinked away the heat in her eyes. "I know he does."

Lily took a deep breath. "So…do you love him?"

Callie felt the weight of admission grasp her shoulders with two hands. She wasn't about to deny it. She wouldn't dishonor what she had shared with Noah by doing that. "Yes… very much."

Lily's jaw clenched with emotion. "But what if it doesn't work out?"

Callie put her arms around Lily's thin shoulders and experienced a fierce burst of protectiveness inside her chest. "What if it does?"

Lily swallowed hard and flashed defiant eyes at her as she pulled away. "You don't know that. People leave all the time."

"Not all people," Callie assured her.

Lily shrugged but Callie wasn't fooled. She was in tremendous pain.

"Yeah, well, I know Dad said I could come back here for lessons, but I think I'll stick with Janelle." Lily lifted her chin, patted Samson one more time and pushed herself away from the fence. "She's a pretty good teacher after all. And she's got way better horses than you."

She took off and Callie gave her a lead of fifty feet before following. When she reached Noah, Lily was already tucked inside the truck with her bicycle in the back.

Another car had turned into the driveway. Her four o'clock appointment.

"I'll call you," he said quietly.

"Sure. Noah…" Her words trailed and she waited for him to respond.

He did. "I'm trying to give you space, Callie. I'm trying to understand everything you've been through and how hard it is for you to trust me, to trust *us*. But at some point you're going to have to meet me halfway. When you're ready for that, give me a call."

He walked off. There was no touch. No kiss. Only the sound of his truck disappearing over the gravel as he drove off.

Halfway. She was still thinking about his words the following afternoon. And trust. It didn't take a genius to figure the two things went hand in hand. Callie left Joe in charge of bedding the horses down for the night and headed into Bellandale. She stopped at a popular Mexican restaurant and ordered takeout, then drove back toward Crystal Point. By the time she pulled up outside Noah's house it was past five o'clock. An unfamiliar flashy-looking blue car was out front, parked next to Noah's truck.

Harry came off his usual spot on the porch and ambled toward her as she unloaded the plastic carry bags containing the food. She was a few steps from the porch when the front opened and Officer Cameron Jakowski stepped outside.

He flashed a too-brilliant smile when he saw her. "Hey, Callie."

"Hi. Is Noah—"

"On the phone," he supplied, rattling his keys. "Hey, I was going to call you."

He was? For what? "Really?"

"I have some news about your recent entanglement with the law." He was smiling and she relaxed.

Apparently the men who'd rammed her trailer had pleaded guilty and were due for a hearing in front of the local magistrate. Cameron suspected they'd get a suspended sentence, but Callie hoped it would at least be enough to stop them from doing anything that stupid again. She told him her insurance had covered the repairs to her trailer.

She said goodbye to Cameron and waited until he'd driven off before she headed inside the house. She could hear Noah's voice and followed the sound until she reached the kitchen. He stood by the counter and had his back to her, the telephone cradled against his ear. He still wore his work clothes and the perfectly tailored chinos did little to disguise the body beneath. Callie's heart hammered behind her ribs just thinking about it.

He turned immediately and looked surprised to find her in his kitchen. He quickly ended the call. "I didn't expect to see you tonight."

She held the bags in front of her. "I brought dinner," she said and placed the bags and her tote on the granite top.

"Don't you have a competition tomorrow?"

Callie nodded. "I do. But I thought dinner might be a good idea." She tried to sound cheerful. "Where are the kids?"

"With my mother."

Callie looked at the large quantity of food she'd bought. "Oh."

"They'll be home in an hour."

"And Lily?"

He didn't move. He didn't break eye contact. "At Maddy's, as usual."

Callie was concerned for his daughter. "Is she okay?"

"She's quiet," he replied. "But Lily gets like that."

Callie took a couple of steps toward him. "She was upset the other day. I tried to talk with her…but I don't know if I got through. She said she didn't want to come back to Sandhills."

"Lily doesn't know what she wants." He pushed himself away from the counter. "She likes you but doesn't want to admit it."

The irony in his words weren't missed. Hadn't he said the same thing about their relationship only yesterday? She'd come to his house to talk, to explain. It was time to open up.

She pulled out a chair and sat down at the table. "Halfway."

"What?"

"That's why I'm here. Yesterday you said I needed to meet you halfway. So, I'm here." She drew in a breath. "Halfway."

"Callie, I—"

"You know, all my life I've pretty much done what I wanted," she said quietly. "I left school at seventeen—I didn't even finish senior year. I wanted to ride. I wanted to be with Craig. And nothing could have stopped me from realizing my dream. Looking back, I was quite self-indulgent. But then I got pregnant and my life changed. Suddenly it wasn't just about me."

"Kids do change your priorities."

Callie nodded. "And I wanted the baby. Having Ryan was the most incredible gift. Even though he only lived for two days I will treasure those moments forever."

"You should, Callie," he said, with such gentleness. "You *should* celebrate his life."

"And get on with my own, is that what you mean?" She sighed heavily. "I want to. And I am trying. Despite how it might seem, I *have* accepted the fact I'll probably never have children. I know people can live full and meaningful lives without having kids."

"But?"

Moisture sprang into her eyes. "But I met you. And you have these incredible children who look at me with such… hope." Tears hovered on her lashes. "I know what they want. I know what they need. And I certainly know what they deserve. But because of Ryan…because I feel so much hurt…I don't know if I could ever give it to them. I don't know if I could ever feel what they would need me to feel."

He looked at her in that way no one else ever had. "Because you didn't carry them? Because you didn't give birth to them?"

She nodded, ashamed of her feelings but unable to deny the truth of them. "Partly, yes."

He stepped closer, bridging the gap. "Do you really think genetics make a parent, Callie?"

She shrugged, without words, without voice.

"What about all the adopted kids out there, the fostered kids, the babies born to a surrogate—do you think their parents love them less because they carry different blood?" His eyes never left hers. "Blood doesn't make you a parent."

"I know it sounds…selfish. It sounds self-absorbed and I'm ashamed to have these kinds of feelings. But, Noah, you have four children who—"

"One," he said quietly, silencing her immediately. "I have one child."

Chapter Twelve

Noah saw her shock and felt the heaviness of his admittance crush right down between his shoulder blades.

"What?"

"I have one *biological* child," he said with emphasis. "I have two who I know definitely aren't mine, another who might not be."

"But Lily—"

"Is mine," he said. "The twins, no...Jamie, I'm not sure."

She looked staggered by his admission and he couldn't blame her. "But you love them so much," she whispered incredulously.

He nodded and fought the lump of emotion that suddenly formed in his throat. "Of course I do. They are *mine*, Callie, despite how they were conceived. That's what I'm trying to say to you—it doesn't matter how they came into the world. What matters is how they are raised, nurtured, loved."

She nodded and he hoped she believed him. He loved her

so much and wanted to share his life with her and marry her as soon as she was ready. He wanted to ask her now. He wanted to drop to his knees and worship her and beg her to become his wife. But he knew they could only have that if she was prepared to accept his children as her own.

"And you're sure the twins aren't yours?"

"Yeah. Margaret took off to Paris to visit her mother and when she came back announced she was pregnant with twins. I knew straight away they weren't mine."

"You did?"

"I'd stopped sleeping with her a long time before. When I suspected she was cheating," he admitted, "I stuck it out for as long as I could for the kids. But I knew the day would come when we'd split. Margaret's moods were unpredictable. Looking back I'm certain she suffered from some kind of depression."

"What did you do?"

"I said I wanted a divorce. I was prepared to let her have the house, but I demanded joint custody." He moved to the table and pulled out a chair. "But instead she walked out after the twins were born. I think she knew, on some level, that leaving them was the best thing she could do for them. She just didn't want them."

"And Jamie?"

He sat down. "She told me the morning she left. That she wasn't sure if he was my son."

"You must have been devastated." Callie grabbed his hand and held on tight.

He nodded, remembering the shock and disbelief he'd experienced. "For about ten seconds I thought I'd been robbed of my son. But that feeling didn't last. He's my child in every way that counts. Just as the twins are."

"Does anyone know?"

"Cameron knows. My parents. Evie. And you."

"Do you think you'll ever tell them?"

He shrugged. "I'm not sure. Perhaps when they're older and can comprehend what it means."

He'd thought about it. Wondered how he would ever broach the subject with them.

"They'll understand," she said softly. "They love you."

"And that's really all it takes, Callie."

Callie knew he was right. And when the kids returned home a little while later and raced toward her with hugs full of unbridled excitement she couldn't control the urge to hug them back. Noah's parents stayed for dinner of reheated fajitas, enchiladas and refried beans, and it was such a delightfully animated and loving evening Callie was tempted to ask Noah to go and collect Lily so she could be part of it.

He was an amazing man. He cherished children that weren't his own. But Craig hadn't wanted his own child.

How could I have loved two men who were so very different?

Callie knew she had to let go of her hurt over Craig. And strangely, as though she'd willed it from sheer thought, her anger, the bitterness she'd clung onto, drifted off.

I don't hate Craig anymore.

It felt good to release all the bad feelings that had been weighing her down. And to know she could love again…to know she *did* love again…filled her with an extraordinary sense of peace. But Callie knew she had one more thing to do. One more hurdle to take. The hardest thing of all was ahead of her. It was something she had to do before she could completely let herself love and be loved.

I have to say goodbye to Ryan.

And the only place she could do that was in California.

The following day Callie called her mother, booked her flight for Wednesday evening, and arranged for Joe to stay at the farm for the time she would be away.

She hadn't stayed at Noah's the previous night. Instead, she'd gone home and stared at the ceiling. She hadn't told him of her plans. She was going to his home on Monday night and she would explain it to him. And she prayed he would understand.

On Monday afternoon Angela Spears arrived with Maddy. The young girl flew from the Lexus with lightning speed and showed Callie her cast. There was no lesson for Maddy, but she wanted to pet Sunshine and spend time with the horses.

Both women were surprised to see Noah's truck pull into the driveway and park beside Angela's Lexus.

The kids jumped out, headed straight for Callie and hugged her tightly. Hayley grabbed her hand and Angela didn't miss a thing.

"Goodness, you're popular," she said good-humoredly and looked toward Noah. "With everyone."

Callie blushed and turned her attention to the man who stood smiling. "I didn't expect you this afternoon. Are we still on for tonight?"

He nodded. "Of course. I'm here to pick up Lily," he said. "Is she with that horse?"

Callie shook her head. "Lily's not here."

He frowned. "What do you mean, she's not here?" His gaze snapped toward Angela. "She told me this morning that you'd bring her here this afternoon so I could pick her up."

Angela's face prickled with concern. "I haven't seen Lily since yesterday."

Callie looked at Noah. She saw the alarm in his eyes. "I'm sure she's somewhere close," Callie said quickly. "Perhaps she's with Evie."

"We just left Evie's."

"Well, your parents? Or Mary-Jayne?" she suggested, trying to sound hopeful. "Call them."

He did that while Callie questioned Jamie, but he said he

had no idea where she was. However, he did say he'd noticed her big backpack was missing and her iPod.

"No luck," he said after a few minutes. "I'll try her cell."

It was switched off. Angela called for Maddy and the teenager came toward them swiftly. She stood in front of her mother, wide-eyed, as if sensing the adults around her were on high alert.

"Madison," Angela said quietly. "Do you know where Lily is?"

"I—um…"

"Maddy?" Noah's voice, calm, deep. "Please…where is she?"

Maddy's eyes filled with tears. "I told her not to," she said. "I said she shouldn't do it. But she wouldn't listen to me."

"What do you mean, Madison?" Angela again, in formidable mother mode.

"When she didn't come to school today I knew she had really done it." Maddy took a huge gulp of air. "She's gone."

Gone. Callie's stomach sank. She clutched Noah's arm instinctively.

Noah took a heavy breath. "Where's she gone, Maddy?"

Maddy swallowed, looked to the ground, then back at her mother and clearly knew she had little choice but to tell the truth. "Paris."

Callie was certain their hearts stopped beating. Angela looked like she would hyperventilate. Noah paled when the reality of it hit him.

"How's she getting there?" he asked evenly, but Callie wasn't fooled. He was out of his mind with worry.

Tears flowed down Maddy's cheek. "She caught the train to Brisbane this morning. She said she was going to buy a ticket at the airport."

"Surely she wouldn't be able to do that," Angela said, all wide-eyed. "Oh, this is bad, this is—"

"Does she have a passport?" Callie asked, cutting off Angela.

Noah nodded. "Yeah. I took the kids to Hawaii last year."

"Why Paris?" Angela asked.

Callie looked at Noah. She knew why, as he did. But it was Maddy Spears who spoke.

"She wants to see her mother."

Callie got Noah into the house so they could make the appropriate telephone calls. She settled the kids in the kitchen with a snack and returned to the living room. Angela left with Maddy, but insisted she'd do whatever was needed to help.

Noah was on the phone, obviously to Cameron by the cryptic conversation. When he hung up he called Evie and instructed her to fill their parents in on the details. "Cameron's going to get her picture to the airport security," he said when he'd hung up.

"That should help," she said. "Is there anything I can do?"

He nodded. "Watch the kids. I have to get to the city as fast as I can," he said. He unclipped his keys and left one by the telephone. "House key," he said. "They'd probably prefer to sleep in their own beds."

Callie didn't hesitate to agree. "I'll take them home soon. You just…go…and call me when you know anything."

"Thanks." He ran a hand across his face. "This is my fault," he said. "I should have paid more attention. She's been quiet since…"

"Since she saw you here last week?"

He nodded and Callie saw the concern in his eyes. She knew what he was thinking, fearing. There were dangers in the big city, people who did bad things, predators waiting to pounce on a naïve young girl from a small town. She rallied instead. "She'll be fine. And she'll be found before you know it." She took a few steps toward him and placed her hands on his chest. "You have to believe that, Noah. For your own peace of mind."

She hugged him close and then watched as he drove off, waiting until she saw the taillights fade before she closed the door. The kids were relaxed enough in her company that they barely questioned their father's quick departure. Jamie talked to her about Lily, though, and because he was such a sensitive child she tried to put his fears at ease the best she could.

She left Joe to bed the horses down for the night, packed a small overnight bag, collected the children and Tessa and took them home.

Noah drove faster than he should have. A flight would have been sensible, but none would have gotten him to Brisbane airport in better time. Thankful that he had a full tank of gas, he drove straight through the four-and-a-half-hour trip without stopping. It was nine-thirty when he raced into the international terminal. He headed directly for airport security and, despite his impatience, was appreciative of their assistance.

"We have her picture here," a female officer told him. "But so far no one matching this description has shown up."

"Her train got in hours ago," Noah told them. "She has to be here somewhere."

"She can't pass this point unless she has a ticket," she assured him.

"Is there any chance she might get one?" he asked, his heart pumping.

"No," the officer said confidently. "The airlines are not in the habit of allowing minors to purchase tickets. You could try the domestic terminal," she said. "If she's resourceful enough, she could think it easier to try for a ticket to Sydney and then perhaps catch a connecting flight."

Noah's head felt like it was about to burst. "I'll go and check." He handed her a business card. "If she turns up here, please call me."

He jumped into a taxi to get to the domestic terminal and once there was scanned by a handheld metal detection device before a uniformed officer led him through. There were plenty of travelers about, browsing the shops; some were sitting in the departure lounges. Noah couldn't see Lily. Panic rose like bile in his throat. What if she wasn't here? What if something had already happened to her? Perhaps she never made it off the train.

He continued his search, checking cafés and a few of the stores that might appeal to a thirteen-year-old girl. He checked every one, showed her picture to as many sales assistants as he could and found some relief when one told him she looked a little familiar.

Fifteen minutes later he was almost out of his mind. He stopped by the escalators and looked up and down the long terminal while the security officer left to check the washrooms. Then just when his hope faded, he noticed a girl, standing alone, looking out of the observation window at the farthest end of the terminal. She had her back to him, and her hair was brown... *Not Lily.*

Noah turned to walk back to the main departure lounge but stopped. He had another look, longer this time. And suddenly his feet were moving toward her. Something about the way she held her shoulders, the angle of her head as she gazed out toward the runway and watched the departing aircraft niggled at him. The departure gates at this end of the terminal were all shut down for the night and she seemed oddly out of place in her solitude.

He kept walking, faster until he was almost at a jog. He halted about thirty feet from her. He noticed details within seconds. She wore a denim skirt and white top. Lily only wore black. And the hair—wrong color completely. And the shoes—not her trademark Doc Martens, but bright pink flip-flops with sequins sewn on them.

But there was a backpack at her feet. Lily's backpack. "Lily?"

She turned and Noah's jaw nearly dropped to his feet. No dark makeup, no piercings, just his daughter's beautiful face staring at him.

"Dad!"

Noah wasn't sure what to expect from her. He didn't have to wait long. She ran toward him and threw herself against him with a sturdy thump. *I have my kid. She's safe.*

"I'm sorry, Dad," she choked the words into his shoulder.

"It's okay." Noah touched her hair. "You scared me to death, Lily."

"I know…I'm so sorry."

"Come and sit down," he said to Lily.

She sat in one of the chairs and Noah retrieved her back-pack.

"You travel light," he said, dropping it at her feet. He sat down beside her. "What are you doing here?"

She shrugged and inhaled a shaky breath. "I'm not sure."

"Maddy said you were going to find your mother," he said, gently because he sensed that was all she could cope with. "Is that true?"

Another shrug, this time accompanied by tears. "No. Yes."

Noah felt her pain right through to his bones. "Why now?"

"I wanted to ask her something."

Noah held his breath for a moment. "Do you know where she lives?"

Lily shook her head.

"How did you plan to find her once you got to Paris?" he asked.

She dropped her gaze. "I've got Grandma's address."

Noah could only imagine what seventy-four-year-old Leila would think about having Lily turn up at her door. "So what did you want to ask your mother?"

She shrugged again. "What we did. What *I* did."

"What you did?"

"To make her not want us."

Noah sighed and chose his words carefully. "You didn't do anything, Lily. Your mother was unhappy. And she didn't want to be married to me. But *you*," he took her hand and squeezed. "You didn't do anything. I promise."

"It feels like she left because of me. I mean, it couldn't have been the others—they were little. And everyone loves little kids."

"It wasn't you," he said again, firmer this time. "Lily, is this really about your mother, or is it Callie?"

Lily looked at him. Her bottom lip quivered and her gaze fell to the floor.

"Are you afraid she'll try to replace your mother?" he asked gently.

Lily turned her face into his shoulder and sobbed against him. "That's just it, Dad," she said brokenly. "I really want her to be replaced. Sometimes I forget what she'd looked like. Jamie doesn't even remember her—it's like she never existed."

"She did exist," Noah said, holding her. "You're proof of that."

Lily hiccupped. "But she left. We weren't enough for her. None of us. If she didn't love us enough to stay…why would someone else? She had to love us, and even that wasn't enough. And Callie, well, she wouldn't *have* to love us, would she? So I thought if I just asked her what made her leave, I could make sure it didn't happen again so that Callie…so that Callie wouldn't leave us, too."

Noah felt pain rip through his chest. Pain for the child

he held in his arms. And he understood, finally. Lily's fears weren't that another woman would come into their life and try to replace the mother she knew. She was afraid another woman might leave them in the same painful fashion.

He pulled back and made her look at him. "You know, Lily, there are no guarantees in any relationship. But if you trust me—you'll trust that I'll always do what's right by you and your sister and brothers."

"I do trust you, Dad," she said, hugging him. "I love you."

"I love you too, kid."

"I'm sorry I ran off," she said, smiling now, even though tears remained in her eyes. "I know you were worried. But I don't think I would have gotten on the plane. I was standing here before, thinking about you and Jamie and the twins and Aunt Evie and everyone else, and thought I'd miss everyone so much if I left. And I'd miss Maddy and Callie and Samson."

Emotion closed his throat. "And I'd miss you, Lily."

"Besides," she said with a sniff, "it's my birthday next week."

Enough said. "Okay. How about we get out of here?"

She reached for her backpack. "So, Dad, you haven't said what a dork I look like."

He ruffled her hair. "I think you look pretty."

She laughed. "Well, the hair's pretty cool…but these shoes have gotta go."

Callie spent the night in Noah's bed, wrapped up in the sheets, secure and safe. It was a lovely room. The huge bed was covered in a quilt in neutral beige and moss green, and the timber walls and silky oak furnishings were rich and warm.

He called her just before ten o'clock and told her that he'd found Lily and they were on their way home. He told her not to wait up and she hung up the telephone, missing him, craving him and feeling relieved he'd found his daughter.

Her heart went out to Lily. To all the kids. And to Noah. Being in his house, sleeping in his bed…it made their relationship seem very *real*. Perhaps for the first time since they'd met. And the responsibility of what that meant weighed heavily. Accepting the children into her heart was only a part of it. First her heart, then her life. Saying goodbye to Ryan was the first step.

But then what?

She'd return to Sandhills and everything would still be there, waiting for her.

Including Noah.

Only, a niggling thought lingered in the back of her mind. What if she couldn't say goodbye to her son? What if it was too much, too hard, too…everything. What then? Could she come back and face Noah and the kids, knowing she'd break their hearts into tiny pieces? Bathing the kids, dressing them in their pajamas, laughing over a botched dinner of grilled cheese and cookies had been wonderful. And she enjoyed their company so much. But there was doubt, too. And fear that she wouldn't measure up. They would expect all of her. An expectation they deserved. Did she have enough left inside herself for all that love?

Later that night, with the kids all tucked into their beds, Tessa locked in the laundry room and Harry guarding the front porch, Callie drifted into sleep.

She was quickly dreaming. Dreaming about Noah, about strong arms and warm lips and gentle hands. She could feel his touch; feel the love in his fingertips as he caressed her back and hips. Callie stretched her limbs, feeling him, wanting him.

And then the dream suddenly wasn't a dream. It was

real. She was in his arms, pressed against his chest. "You're here," she murmured into his throat. "You're home. I'm glad. Lily—"

"Shhhh," he said against her hair. "Lily's fine. Go back to sleep."

When Callie awoke a couple of hours later she could hear the rhythmic sound of the bedside clock and Noah's steady breathing. He lay on his stomach, his face turned away from her. She touched his back, rested her hand on him for a few moments and then slipped out of bed as quietly as she could.

When she padded downstairs a few minutes later she heard young voices whispering. The twins were awake, still in their beds but chatting to each other. Jamie emerged as though he had some kind of adult radar and quickly said he was hungry. Lily's door was still closed and Callie knew she'd still be sleeping. Breakfast was as hit-and-miss as dinner the night before, but the kids didn't complain. She gave them cereal and put on a pot of coffee and when they were done Callie herded them back to their rooms with instructions to stay quiet for at least another hour.

When she returned to the upstairs bedroom Noah was lying on his side with his eyes open. She closed the door softly and sat on the bed. "Sorry, did I wake you?"

He sighed wearily. "It was a long night."

"You should have stayed over and driven back this morning."

"I needed to get back."

"The kids were fine. Another few hours wouldn't have made any difference."

He looked at her. "Okay, I *wanted* to get back. As for them being fine," he said quietly and reached for her hand, "I knew they would be." He kissed her wrist and turned her hand over and kissed her knuckles. "In fact, I can't remember the last time the house was so quiet in the morning."

She smiled. "They're under strict instructions to be as quiet as mice for the next hour."

"What about you—don't you have to get back to your horses?"

"Joe will see to them this morning." She touched his face with her free hand. "How's Lily?"

"She's okay. She slept most of the drive home. We had a good talk about things. I think she'll be fine."

Callie had to ask what she feared. "Did she do this because of me? Because of us?"

"Not in the way you might think." He held her hand firm and told her how Lily was feeling. "You know, she's more like you than you realize."

Callie's breath caught in her throat. "In what way?"

Noah smiled lightly. "Impulsive. Sometimes hardheaded. But...extraordinary." He kissed her hand again. "I thought that the first time I met you. Those beautiful eyes of yours were glaring at me from under that big hat." He sighed. "It blew me away."

He shifted and raised himself up. Callie looked at his bare chest and then lower to where the sheet slipped past his hips and flat stomach. Her fingers suddenly itched with the need to touch, to feel, to taste.

"Keep looking at me like that and I'll forget how tired I am."

She colored hotly. What was she thinking? He'd just driven practically ten hours straight and she was leering at him. "You're right," she said and hopped off the bed. "You should hit the shower and have some breakfast when you've had enough sleep. I'll make sure the twins get to daycare and Jamie gets to school."

Callie sucked in a breath. She had to tell him now. Before she lost her nerve. Before they were any more involved. His name escaped from her lips.

He smiled again and kept his eyes closed. "Hmm."

She took a steadying breath, pushed out some courage and told him of her plans.

"You're going where?" he asked and pulled himself up.

"Los Angeles."

His eyes glittered, narrowing as he took in her words. "Why?" he asked. "Why now?"

Callie saw the confusion on his face. She knew he'd feel this way, knew he'd think her leaving was her way of running, of putting space between them.

Isn't it?

The truth pierced through her. Wasn't she running away? She took another breath.

"Please, Noah, try to understand…" She took his hands. "Please," she said again. "I know it might look like I'm—"

"What?" he said, cutting her off. "Running away? Running out? You forget I know what it feels like to be left, Callie."

She turned her hands in his and held them against his chest. "It's not like that."

He looked at her, deep, way down, like he was trying to absorb her with his eyes. Callie felt his frustration, his confusion, the sense he wanted to believe her but didn't quite know how. "Are you coming back?"

She hesitated and knew Noah felt it deep inside. "I'm… I'm…"

He grabbed her left hand and gently rubbed the ring finger with his thumb. "You know what I want, Callie. You know that I love you and want to be with you—as your friend and lover and husband."

Tears filled her eyes. "I know," she whispered and wrapped her arms around his waist.

"But that's not enough?"

She wanted to rest her head against his chest. "I just… don't know."

Noah pulled back. "Then I guess there's nothing left to say."

Chapter Thirteen

"You don't look so great."

Noah faked a smile. "Thanks."

Evie was never one to hold back her thoughts. "When's Callie due back?"

"I'm not sure." He felt like he had glass in his mouth. Because he had no idea when she was coming back. Or if.

His sister spun around in his kitchen and continued to chop watermelon with a big knife. "The kids are missing her."

So am I...

Noah tensed. He was in no mood for his sister's counsel. He wasn't in a mood for socializing, either. But it was Lily's birthday and the whole family had arrived to celebrate her day. "She'll be back when she's back." *If she comes back...*

"Have you spoken with her?"

"Is there a point to these questions?"

"Just trying to get you to talk," Evie said, raising both brows. "That's not an easy feat these days."

Noah didn't want to talk. He didn't want fake conversation with well-meaning relatives about how he was feeling. His mother had tried, now Evie. He just wanted to lick his wounds in private. He didn't want to talk about Callie. He didn't want to *think* about Callie.

But he remembered her look the night before she'd left. She'd made love with him, so deeply and with such an acute response to his touch it had felt like…it felt like…*goodbye.*

"So have you?"

Evie's voice shuttled Noah quickly back to the present. "Have I what?"

"Talked with her?"

He nodded. "Of course." Not exactly the truth. She'd called him when she'd landed in Los Angeles and he'd heard nothing since.

"Can I ask you something?"

Noah frowned. "Would it make any difference if I said no?"

Evie shrugged. "Probably not."

Noah grabbed the barbecue tongs and fork. "Go ahead."

"Why didn't you go with her?"

He stilled. Evie always knew the wrong question to ask. "Impossible."

"I could have watched the kids," she said. "So, what's your excuse?"

Because she didn't ask me to.

Part of him had longed to go with her, to meet her family, to see where she'd been raised, to be with her. He'd hated the idea of Callie traveling alone. Some base male instinct had kicked in and he wanted to protect her, to keep her safe. He should have insisted. He should have proposed marriage to her like he'd planned to do and taken the trip as an opportunity to meet her mother and brother.

"What's his excuse for what?"

Lily came into the kitchen. Without the gothic makeup and sporting only earrings—no other piercings—and jeans and a T-shirt, she looked so pretty, like a young version of his sister Grace. He smiled as she stole a piece of melon and took a bite.

"Were you guys talking about me?" she asked, suspicious but grinning.

"Of course," Evie said. "What else. How's the head cold?"

"Better," Lily replied. "I'm still sneezing."

Evie passed Lily the plate of fruit. "Well, if you're better, go and take this outside. Your Poppy loves watermelon." She looked at Noah. "You might want to light up the barbecue."

Lily was just about out of the room when Jamie raced into the kitchen. "Callie's here! Callie's here!" he said excitedly. "It's her truck coming."

Noah's stomach did a wild leap. He looked at his sister. "It's not possible."

"Go on," Evie said, shooing him out of the kitchen.

Noah headed for the front door, with Jamie and Lily barely feet behind him. Sure enough, Callie's truck was barreling down the long driveway. And it was hitching a horse trailer.

He opened the screen door. Lily was beside him instantly. So was Evie.

But it wasn't Callie behind the wheel. It was Joe. The skinny youth got out of the truck as Noah took the steps. He could feel Lily in his wake.

"Hi, there," Joe said. "Got a delivery."

Lily gripped Noah's arm. "Dad?"

He shrugged. "I don't know."

By now Evie and Mary-Jayne and his parents were standing by the front steps, with the twins squeezing between them, while Jamie jumped up and down excitedly.

Joe disappeared to the rear of the trailer and lowered the

tailgate. Lily's grip tightened when they saw the solid chestnut gelding step down from the trailer.

"Samson," she whispered. "Dad...look."

"I see him."

Joe led the horse around the truck and held the rope out to an astonished Lily. His daughter took the lead and buried her face in the animal's neck.

Joe pulled an envelope from his pocket and handed it to Lily. "Callie said to give this to you." He shook Noah's hand. "Well, I'll be seeing ya."

They waited until the truck pulled out from the driveway before Lily looked at the card inside. She read it out loud. *Dear Lily, I wish I was there with you. Happy birthday! Love, Callie.*

Tears welled in his daughter's eyes and tipped over her cheeks. "Oh, Dad." She hugged the horse. "I can't believe Callie did this."

Noah couldn't believe it, either. The woman he loved had given his daughter the one thing she longed for. It was an incredible gesture toward Lily. He ached inside thinking about it.

Lily didn't stop crying. "He's mine, he's really mine?"

"It looks that way."

Evie looked at Noah and raised her brows. "Some gift," she said.

Within minutes Lily had led the horse into the small pasture behind the house.

"That's one happy kid," his father said.

His parents had returned to the pool area with the kids and Evie pushed Noah to start up the barbecue. He was just flicking up the heat when Lily rushed through the back door and let it bang with a resounding thud.

"Dad!"

Her stricken look alarmed him and he set the utensils aside. "What is it?"

Lily shook her head frantically. "I want to call Callie."

Noah checked his watch. "Later tonight."

"I want to call her now," Lily insisted. "I want to call her and say thank you. And I want to tell her we miss her and want her to come home."

"You can't do that."

Lily tugged on his arm. "Why not?"

"Because you just can't."

Lily rolled her eyes. "No offense, Dad, but that sounds really dumb."

He shrugged, although he wasn't sure how he moved.

"So, you're not going to do anything?"

His back stiffened. "What exactly do you want me to do?"

Lily's eyes grew huge. "If you don't want me to call her— then you do it. You call her up and tell her we miss her. Tell her *you* miss her. She said in the card that she wished she was here—so call her up and tell her to come back."

Everyone stared at him. Evie raised her eyes questioningly.

He took a deep breath. "I can't tell Callie how to live her life." Another breath. "She's gone to see her family."

Tears filled Lily's eyes again. "I thought…I thought *we* were her family. So if she wants to be with her family she should be here, because *we* live here, *you* live here."

Noah wished he could stop his daughter's relentless logic. "She'll be back when she's ready."

Lily scowled. "Are you sure? What if she changes her mind? What if she stays there?"

Noah had spent the past week thinking of little else. He'd thought about it every night when he laid in his bed, twisting in sheets that still held the scent of her perfume in them. He missed her so much, wanted her so much he hurt all over.

"It's not up to me," he said quietly.

Lily hopped on her feet. "That doesn't make much sense. You love her, right?"

Eight sets of eyes zoomed in on him and he felt their scrutiny. "Well...I—"

"And she loves you," Lily said quickly. "She told me."

Noah rocked back on his heels. "She told you that?"

Lily looked at him like he needed a brain transplant. "I just don't get adults. You give all these lectures about being honest and then you can't even be honest with yourself." She puffed out a breath. "Why don't you just call her up and ask her to marry you?"

Noah's jaw almost fell to his feet. "What happened to your fifty percent of second marriages end in divorce speech?"

Lily swung her arm around. "Who listens to me? What do I know?" Lily blurted. "You guys are the grown-ups—work it out."

He saw Evie nodding. "Don't start," he warned his sister.

"She's got a point."

"Of course I've got a point," Lily said through her tears. "Callie loves you. You love Callie. We all love Callie."

"Yeah, Daddy, we love Callie," Jamie piped in, suddenly next to his sister. The twins weren't far away, either. And his parents hovered nearby.

She really does love me... She told my kid she loves me.

But she left.

And then, with a jolt, he realized he'd been so angry, so hurt, he hadn't really listened when she'd tried to explain. He'd cut her off, his ego dented, his heart smashed.

If he'd really listened he might have heard something other than his own lingering bitterness chanting inside his head. He might have heard that she needed to go home to lay her ghosts to rest.

Suddenly Noah understood. The past—Callie needed to

face her past, come full circle and deal with the grief of losing her fiancé and her son.

He felt the kick of truth knock against his ribs.

She loves me. He looked at his kids, all watching him, their little faces filled with hope. *She loves them.*

"Then I guess we'd better come up with a plan," he said and smiled when he saw everyone around him nodding.

Callie had been back in her old room for a week. It seemed so small now. And it didn't give her the comfort it once used to. But it was good to be home with her mother, especially since Scott had arrived two days after she had.

Her mother's stucco house was small compared to most in this part of Santa Barbara, but it was neat and her gardens were the envy of the neighborhood. She walked into the kitchen for a late breakfast and discovered her brother burning sourdough toast.

"Don't say anything," he cautioned. "I can still cook better than you."

Callie tapped him on the arm. "Ha, so you say."

She took the strawberry cream cheese from the refrigerator and waited while he scraped the burnt offering with a knife. Once he was done he passed it to her. Callie smeared it with spread and sat down.

"So, Mom said you're thinking of taking some time off?"

He shrugged. "Maybe."

"Because of what happened?"

Scott didn't like to discuss the tragic death of a friend and colleague a few months earlier. But she suspected the event had taken its toll on her brother.

"I don't know what I'm doing just yet."

"But you're not thinking of leaving the fire department, right?"

He shrugged. "Like I said, I haven't decided."

"You've wanted to be a fireman since you were four years old."

Scott grinned. "And you wanted to be a vet."

Callie shrugged and bit her bagel. "Nah—not smart enough."

"You could go back to school," he suggested. "Mom said you always got good grades. Not that I remember, being so much younger than you."

Callie held up three fingers. "That's how many years. Hardly worth mentioning."

He grinned again. "So would you?"

"I like my job. And I'm happy."

"Are you? You don't seem so happy to me."

Callie rolled her eyes. "Look who's talking."

"Well I never said I was happy," he replied. "So, what gives?" He smiled and ruffled her hair. "Why this sudden trip home?"

"I wanted to see you and Mom."

"And?"

And I'm in love...and I miss him so much I can hardly breathe. All I want is to go home and run into Noah's arms and stay there for the rest of my life.

"Stop badgering your sister."

Their mother came into the kitchen, a striking, willowy figure in a multicolored silk caftan, who looked much younger than her fifty-five years.

"Just asking," Scott said and grabbed another piece of bread. "You have to admit she showed up out of the blue. It makes me wonder what she's up to."

Callie placed her hands on her hips. "I am in the room, you know."

Scott chuckled. "So, spill."

She held her shoulders stiff. "I have nothing to say."

He bit into a bagel. "She's definitely hiding something."

Eleanor scolded her son and told him to take the dog for a walk. Still grinning, he grabbed his toast and left.

"Is he right?" her mother asked once the back door banged shut.

Callie nodded.

"A man?" Eleanor guessed correctly.

She nodded again.

Her mother sat down and swooshed the swirl of fabric around her legs. "I thought you might have changed," Eleanor said gently.

"Changed how?"

"I thought your time away might have loosened the tight control you've always had on what's inside you."

Callie knew what her mother meant. "I'm not good at talking about this stuff."

But she was with Noah. Callie had shared more with him than she had with anyone. Her heart, her body...all of herself.

"That's why things hurt you so much, Calliope. Even when you were a little girl you never talked about how you were feeling. You were always so happy on the outside. But I worried about you, keeping your feelings in. Your dad was like that, too." Eleanor pushed her bangs from her face. "After his accident, when he was really sick and knew he was dying, he didn't let me know how bad it was until the end."

"I remember."

"That hurt me for a long time," Eleanor admitted. "I thought he didn't trust me."

"He loved you, though. And you loved him."

"Of course," her mother said. "But when someone loves you, you should give them your whole heart."

"Like I did with Craig? That didn't turn out so great."

Eleanor raised her brows questioningly. "Craig was self-absorbed. And you were very young when you met. Had you met him now, as a woman, you probably would have seen right through his lack of integrity. He never deserved you, Callie...but if you've met someone who does, what are you doing here in my kitchen?" Her mother didn't wait for a reply and didn't hold back. "Do you love this man?"

Callie nodded. "I...yes."

Eleanor smiled. "Good. Because he called me yesterday."

"Noah called *you?*" Callie couldn't hide the shock in her voice.

"Mmm. We had a nice long talk about you."

Callie almost spluttered the coffee she'd just sipped. "What?"

"I liked him very much."

Callie was aghast. Why on earth would Noah want to talk with her mother? "Why didn't he call *me?*"

Eleanor widened her bright blue eyes. "Did you give him reason to?"

Did she? "Well, I didn't say he *couldn't* call me." She put down her coffee. Curiosity burned through her. "What did he say?"

Eleanor lifted her shoulders dramatically. "Oh, this and that. He asked how you were doing."

Callie's skin heated. "And what did you tell him?"

"Oh, this and that."

"Mom...please?"

Her mother stood up. "Come for a walk with me in the garden."

Callie followed her mother out the back door and across the lawn toward the small wooden bench in the far corner. They sat in front of a tiny rose garden her mother tended to daily.

"This is my favorite spot," her mother said as she arranged her housecoat on the bench.

Callie sat beside her and looked at the beautiful deep burgundy rosebush just about to bloom. "Dad's flower."

Eleanor smiled. "Not just that." She pointed to a small miniature rose shrub with tiny yellow buds on it. "That one is for my grandson."

Ryan's rose. Of course her mother would do that. Callie grasped her mother's hand. "Thank you, Mom." Callie sighed. "You know, I never thought I'd feel whole again. After Ryan died I shut myself off from everything." She looked at her mother. "And everyone."

She took a long, shuddering breath. "And then one morning Lily Preston knocked on my door and my life changed."

"Kids do that," her mother said fondly. "So does love."

He mother was so right and Callie didn't know whether she should laugh or cry. "The children are incredible. And they…they need me."

"So why are you here?"

Callie looked at the rose planted in her son's memory and said a silent prayer and thank you to the precious baby she'd never forget. And slowly the pain began to ease. She thought about Craig, and there was no anger, no lingering resentment for a man she now realized was never who she'd believed him to be. She felt sad for him. Sad for the time lost. But that was all, and it made her feel incredibly free. She thought about Noah loving children who weren't biologically his and knew he was right—blood and genetics were merely words. And Fiona—forced to give up her baby and living with the belief and hope that her child was being loved and cherished. And she knew, as her heart filled with a heady joy at what the future promised, that loving Noah was the greatest gift she could give his children.

"Why am I here?" Callie echoed her mother's words. "I'm letting go of the past."

"Are you about done?"

Callie nodded. "I'm done. I need to go home now." She

squeezed her mother's hand. "Will you come with me, Mom? I'd like you to meet Noah…and the…and my…"

"Your kids?"

Callie's heart contracted. "Yes."

Eleanor reached across and hugged Callie close. "We're booked to leave tomorrow. That young man of yours can be very persuasive."

Callie laughed with delight. "Oh, Mom, don't I know it."

Bellandale airport only accepted small aircraft, so Callie and her mother caught a connecting flight with a small domestic airline and because of the time difference arrived late Tuesday afternoon.

The airplane hit the runway and took a few minutes to come to a complete stop. Stairs were placed near the door and Callie felt the warm morning air hit her the moment she stepped out into the sunshine.

It was good to be back. And she couldn't wait to see Noah and the children. Fiona was picking them up and Callie intended to go directly to his house to surprise him. She clutched her cabin bag and followed her mother down the steps behind a line of other passengers. The walk across the tarmac took no time at all and when they reached the terminal and walked through the automatic doors the strong rush of the air conditioner was a welcome relief.

People disbursed in front of them, some greeting waiting relatives, some linking up with rental cars or taxis. Callie looked around for the familiar face of her friend and then stopped dead in her tracks as the throng of people in front of her disappeared.

For a moment she couldn't move. Couldn't speak. Couldn't think. She dropped her bag to her feet. Then, through the blur of tears she knew it was true.

Callie saw Lily first, then Jamie, then the twins. Lily held up a sign, as did Jamie, and the little ones had a hand each on a wide piece of cardboard. It spelled three words.

Please... Marry... Us...

The kids all looked hopeful. And Lily—looking so naturally beautiful with her newly colored hair and clean face, stared at her with luminous green eyes that shone brightly with tears. Jamie was smiling the widest smile she'd ever seen and the twins chuckled with such enchanting mischief she just wanted to hug them close.

I love these kids. I want to love them for the rest of my life. I want to be their mother.

She smiled through her tears and Lily came forward and hugged her so tight Callie thought she might break something. "Thank you for my birthday present," Lily said breathlessly. "Please say yes to my dad."

Callie hugged her back as emotion welled inside her. "Where is he?"

"Callie?"

She heard his voice, felt his presence vibrating though her entire body. He was behind her. Callie turned. Her breath caught in her throat. He looked so good. Sounds disappeared, people faded, until there was just him. Only this man she loved so much.

"You're here?" she whispered.

He nodded. "I'm here."

Callie saw Evie and Fiona from the corner of her eye, and watched as they ushered the children toward them and took Eleanor into their inner circle and headed for the exit doors. Noah stepped forward and took her hand. She felt his touch through to every part of her body.

"I can't stand being away from you," he admitted, drawing her closer. "It's killing me."

And right there, in the middle of the airport, with people moving around them, Noah kissed her.

"I'm sorry I left you," she managed to say, when the kissing stopped and she could draw a breath. "I know my reasons didn't make a lot of sense to you. But I had something I had to do before I could give you...all of my heart."

Noah held her in the circle of his arms. "What did you have to do?"

"I had to say goodbye to Ryan."

He swallowed hard and Callie saw the emotion glittering in his green eyes. "I understand."

"I'll always cherish him," she said, holding on to Noah, vaguely aware that people around them were dwindling to just a few. "But I knew I had to let go of all my anger toward Craig and my grief over losing Ryan. I guess it came down to this fear I had of messing up...of not being able to feel what I knew your children deserved me to feel."

"And did you let it go?"

Callie nodded. "Yes—once I realized that I *wanted* to love the kids and that I wanted to be part of their life."

Noah held her hands in front of his chest. "You know what it means, Callie? The whole deal—forever."

"I know what it means," she said on a rush of breath. "I want forever. I want the kids. I want you." She looked into his eyes. *"I love you."*

"It's about time," he breathed into her hair. He kissed her, the sweetest kiss she'd ever known.

"Thank you for not giving up on me," she whispered between kisses.

He held her in his arms. "I never will. Marry me, Callie? I need you. We need you."

She nodded. "Yes," she said, her gaze filled with love. "Yes, I will. I love you," she whispered. "I love you."

"Marry me soon."

"Mmm," she agreed through kisses. "Soon. How about Christmas Eve?"

He smiled against her mouth. "That soon? Good." He reached into his pocket and pulled out a small box. "Because I've been carrying this around with me for days."

Callie stared at the box as he flipped the lid. Inside lay the most beautiful ring she'd ever seen—a gorgeous champagne diamond surrounded by a cluster of pure white stones. She looked at the ring, then Noah. "It's beautiful."

He slipped the ring on her finger and it fit perfectly.

"The kids helped me pick it out." He kissed her forehead gently. "I love you, Callie." He lifted her chin and tilted her head. "And if you ever want to explore that ten-percent chance and look at trying to have a baby—then that's what we'll do. Whatever you decide, I'll be beside you."

Callie felt fresh tears behind her eyes. "Thank you for that. We'll see what happens. For the moment…I just want to learn how to be the best mother I can be to your children."

"Our children now," he said softly. "Maybe we should head outside and break the news?" he suggested and pointed toward the long glass windows and the sea of eager and clearly happy faces watching them.

She nodded and he linked their hands and they walked outside together. As soon as they hit the pavement Lily raced forward and hugged her close and Jamie and the twins followed her lead. With her mother, Evie and Fiona smiling, the kids laughing and hugging and Noah holding her hand so tightly she felt the connection through to her soul, any doubts disappeared. This was what she was made for. This man. This family. Her family.

* * * * *

HEART & HOME

Heartwarming romances where love can
happen right when you least expect it.

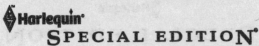

COMING NEXT MONTH
AVAILABLE JANUARY 31, 2012

#2167 FORTUNE'S VALENTINE BRIDE
The Fortunes of Texas: Whirlwind Romance
Marie Ferrarella

#2168 THE RETURN OF BOWIE BRAVO
Bravo Family Ties
Christine Rimmer

#2169 JACKSON HOLE VALENTINE
Rx for Love
Cindy Kirk

#2170 A MATCH MADE BY CUPID
The Foster Brothers
Tracy Madison

#2171 ALMOST A HOMETOWN BRIDE
Helen R. Myers

#2172 HIS MOST IMPORTANT WIN
Cynthia Thomason

You can find more information on upcoming Harlequin® titles,
free excerpts and more at www.HarlequinInsideRomance.com.

HSECNM0112

REQUEST YOUR FREE BOOKS!

2 FREE NOVELS PLUS 2 FREE GIFTS!

✦ Harlequin®

SPECIAL EDITION

Life, Love & Family

Discover a touching new trilogy from
USA TODAY bestselling author

Janice Kay Johnson

Between Love and Duty

As the eldest brother of three, Duncan MacLachlan
is used to being in control and maintaining an
emotional distance; as a police captain it's his job.
But when he meets Jane Brooks, Duncan soon finds
his control slipping away. Together, they fight for a
young boy's future, and soon Duncan finds himself
hoping to build a future with Jane.

Available February 2012

From Father to Son
(March 2012)

The Call of Bravery
(April 2012)

Louisa Morgan loves being around children.
So when she has the opportunity to tutor bedridden Ellie,
she's determined to bring joy back into the motherless
girl's world. Can she also help Ellie's father open his
heart again? Read on for a sneak peek of

THE COWBOY FATHER

by Linda Ford,
available February 2012 from Love Inspired Historical.

Why had Louisa thought she could do this job? A bubble of self-pity whispered she was totally useless, but Louisa ignored it. She wasn't useless. She could help Ellie if the child allowed it.

Emmet walked her out, waiting until they were out of earshot to speak. "I sense you and Ellie are not getting along."

"Ellie has lost her freedom. On top of that, everything is new. Familiar things are gone. Her only defense is to exert what little independence she has left. I believe she will soon tire of it and find there are more enjoyable ways to pass the time."

He looked doubtful. Louisa feared he would tell her not to return. But after several seconds' consideration, he sighed heavily. "You're right about one thing. She's lost everything. She can hardly be blamed for feeling out of sorts."

"She hasn't lost everything, though." Her words were quiet, coming from a place full of certainty that Emmet was more than enough for this child. "She has you."

"She'll always have me. As long as I live." He clenched his fists. "And I fully intend to raise her in such a way that even if something happened to me, she would never feel like I was gone. I'd be in her thoughts and in her actions every day."

Peace filled Louisa. "Exactly what my father did."

Their gazes connected, forged a single thought about fathers and daughters…how each needed the other. How sweet the relationship was.

Louisa tipped her head away first. "I'll see you tomorrow."

Emmet nodded. "Until tomorrow then."

She climbed behind the wheel of their automobile and turned toward home. She admired Emmet's devotion to his child. It reminded her of the love her own father had lavished on Louisa and her sisters. Louisa smiled as fond memories of her father filled her thoughts. Ellie was a fortunate child to know such love.

Louisa understands what both father and daughter are going through. Will her compassion help them heal—and form a new family? Find out in
THE COWBOY FATHER
by Linda Ford, available February 14, 2012.

Love Inspired Books celebrates 15 years of inspirational romance in 2012! February puts the spotlight on Love Inspired Historical, with each book celebrating family and the special place it has in our hearts. Be sure to pick up all four Love Inspired Historical stories, available February 14, wherever books are sold.

SHLIHEXP0212

USA TODAY bestselling author

Sarah Morgan

brings readers another enchanting story

ONCE A FERRARA WIFE...

When Laurel Ferrara is summoned back to Sicily
by her estranged husband, billionaire
Cristiano Ferrara, Laurel knows things are about
to heat up. And Cristiano's power is a potent
reminder of his Sicilian dynasty's unbreakable rule:
once a Ferrara wife, always a Ferrara wife....

Sparks fly this February

HARLEQUIN® HISTORICAL:
Where love is timeless

INTRODUCING
LOUISE ALLEN'S
MOST SCANDALOUS TRILOGY YET!

Danger & Desire

Leaving the sultry shores of India behind them, the passengers of the *Bengal Queen* face a new life ahead in England—until a shipwreck throws their plans into disarray....

Can Alistair and Perdita's illicit onboard flirtation survive the glittering social whirl of London?

Washed up on an island populated by ruffians, virginal Averil must rely on rebel captain Luc for protection....

And honorable Callum finds himself falling for his brother's fiancée!

Take the plunge this February!

Ravished by the Rake
February 2012

Seduced by the Scoundrel
March 2012

Married to a Stranger
April 2012

www.Harlequin.com

HHLA29676